No-See-Me
and the Amazing Crimson Stick

ALSO BY MARY VERDICK

A Place of Honor

The Unexpected Journey

Indian Time

Don't Let the Good Life Pass You By

Maybe This Time

As Long as He Needs Me

That Certain Summer

Another Time, Another Place

No-See-Me
and the Amazing Crimson Stick

Mary Verdick

authorHOUSE®

AuthorHouse™
1663 Liberty Drive
Bloomington, IN 47403
www.authorhouse.com
Phone: 1-800-839-8640

Published by AuthorHouse   01/21/2015

ISBN: 978-1-4969-5848-8 (sc)
ISBN: 978-1-4969-5849-5 (hc)
ISBN: 978-1-4969-5847-1 (e)

Library of Congress Control Number: 2014922104

Any people depicted in stock imagery provided by Thinkstock are models, and such images are being used for illustrative purposes only. Certain stock imagery © Thinkstock.

This book is printed on acid-free paper.

To my grandchildren,

Jennifer and Christian, with love

CHAPTER ONE

They had just finished breakfast, but before he left for work Ben casually asked if she'd heard anything new from her publishers. The author of a popular young adult series entitled, *No-See-Me and the Amazing Crimson Stick,* Meggie had written the first book years ago, almost as a joke, and no one was more surprised than she when it took off. Now, with Ben's encouragement—he'd believed in her from the start—she turned out two or three books a year, and the series had developed into a profitable cottage industry. Her editor routinely updated her on sales and her position on the New York Times best seller list, and she told Ben now that at last count they'd sold another 200,000 copies. The phenomenal sales of the books still shocked her, and she felt secretly that there must be some mistake. But Ben took it all in stride.

"Not surprised. You're a publishing sensational, darling," he said, with his sweet, endearing grin. Then getting to his feet he put his arms around her and hugged her. "Shall we go out tonight and celebrate?"

"Fine with me," she said. And just then the phone rang. She was expecting a call from her editor, who wanted to discuss some changes she'd made in her last story. She picked up the phone. "Hello." But it wasn't her editor.

"Hello, brat," a voice said, and immediately twenty-five years vanished in the wink of an eye. She began to tremble uncontrollably.

"Josh?" She grabbed the back of a straight-back chair to keep from falling. "Is that you? Is it really *you*?"

"In the flesh," he said. "Got back to New York couple of months ago, and I'm coming to a conference in Hartford this afternoon. I was wondering if I could drop by to see you and Ben, hash over old times."

"Of course. That'll be great," she said, swallowing. Turning to her husband she mouthed the words, "Josh Hawkins," and saw his eyes widen in surprise—or was it shock? "Ben and I would love to see you, Josh. How long you going to be in town?"

"Oh, just a few hours. I've rented a car, and if I start now I could be there by ten-thirty or so, if that's convenient."

"Perfect. If you have any trouble finding the house—"

"Oh that won't be a problem. The car's got a GPS."

"Good. We'll look forward to seeing you then."

"Me, too," he said. "It's been a long time, Meggie, girl."

Another lifetime, she thought. Murmuring, "Good-bye," she hung up. Then turning back to Ben, who was looking slightly nonplussed, she said again, "Josh Hawkins. Can you believe it? He's in New York and is coming to Hartford."

"When did he leave Africa?"

"Who knows? Mom didn't say anything about it, and I think they still keep in touch."

"Wonder why he's coming here?"

She shrugged. "Some sort of conference apparently. Want to come home for lunch to see him?"

"Can't." Ben shook his head. "Big corporate meeting this morning—they've got me down for a speech. How 'bout you ask him to dinner?" He gave her a quick kiss and went out to his car.

Standing in the window Meggie watched him drive off. Then glancing down at herself—she was wearing jeans and a T-shirt, her usual at-home attire—she decided that simply wouldn't do. Going to her bedroom she opened her closet and started scanning its contents. What *should* she wear? She wanted to look nice, but not like she was trying to impress him or anything—not that Josh would even notice what she had on probably.

He'd never paid much attention to her clothes, although that wasn't quite true. If she wore something a little too tight, or cut somewhat low in the neck, he never hesitated to tell her what he thought.

"Why flaunt it?" he'd said one night when she was wearing a white silk sheath and pearls that showed off her creamy skin to perfection. The dress was strapless, but not particularly daring, yet Josh acted as if she were half-naked. "I hope you're taking along a shawl to cover that thing up."

"Oh, you!" she wailed, shaking her head. Her light brown hair, shot through with golden threads, fell to her shoulders in waves, and her eyes, big and sparkly, seemed to change color as you looked at them, green to gray and back again. She was a very pretty girl, although she seemed totally unaware of it, which only added to her charm. "What's wrong with this dress?"

"Nothing," Ben Brown said. Ben was short and solid, like his name, with a sprinkling of freckles across his nose and cheeks and a mop of bright red hair. He was officially Josh's friend, but he often took Meggie places when Josh was busy or didn't want to go. Like the party tonight at Mary Beth Evans.

Meggie had a suspicion that Mary Beth, an older girl, had invited her and Josh only because she had a crush on Josh and hoped to snare him by pretending an interest in his little sister. Only Josh was on to her and decided to pass on the invitation.

"But *I* want to go!" Meggie protested. "Mary Beth has this fabulous house, I've been told, with a dance floor that pops up right over the pool and underwater lights and all. It'll be fun—but I can't go by myself. You know I can't!"

"Than I'll ask Ben to take you. He won't mind."

And being Ben he didn't. "Always glad to do a favor," he said. "And, hey, you look really great in that dress, Meg. Why you'll be the best looking gal at the party I bet. Don't listen to your stuffy old brother."

"He's not *really* my brother," she said. Of course she and Josh had lived in the same house for years, ever since her mother had married Josh's father when Meggie was eight and Josh eleven. And their folks might never have gotten married, she thought, if it hadn't been for *No-See-Me and the Amazing Crimson Stick*. Not that she was totally convinced of the Stick's magic. It was just an inanimate object after all, and yet, and yet—as long as she lived she'd never forget the first time the Stick had intervened on her behalf.

She'd been walking to school with Timmy Wysocki, her next door neighbor, who was small and frail, and got picked on a lot. Meggie was aware of her little friend's vulnerability, but she'd never felt particularly protective of him. Until that morning, a glorious, clear cold day when the trees were showing off their autumn colors, fiery reds and newly minted gold and every shade of green imaginable. It was the kind of day when you felt happy just to be alive, and Meggie loved the smell of autumn in the air. But when they reached the school yard they came face to face with big, hulking Cy Barnes, the school bully. Meggie knew of Cy's reputation as king of the hill and had successfully avoided him since school started. But suddenly today there he was, planted squarely in front of them, blocking their path.

"Okay, po'-boy," he sneered at Timmy. "How much dough your sweet mama give you for lunch today?" And he stuck out his palm. "Gimme gimme, hand it over."

To Meggie's astonishment, Timmy, with a look of resignation, reached in his pocket and pulled out several one-dollar bills, which the older boy lost no time grabbing. Well, this was just too much for Meggie. "What's with you, Barnes?" she said. "Just who do you think you are?" And she lunged toward him, only to trip over something lying in her path. It was a stick about a foot long and of a bright crimson color, and as she grabbed it, to keep from falling, it began to shake and a strange exciting tremor started coursing through her body.

"Give Timmy back his money," she ordered Cy, "and leave him alone, you creep. Or I'll report you to the principal and you'll be kicked out of school."

At these words the older boy's face blanched and he said in a small, chastened voice, "Okay, Meg. Gotcha. Okay." He wet his lips, and with shaking hand returned Timmy's money. "Didn't mean no harm," he muttered. "Sorry, Tim, old boy."

"Well, you ought to be," Meggie snapped. "And don't let it happen again or you'll regret it." And amazingly Timmy, and the rest of Cy's victims, had no more trouble with him after that. It was almost as if he became a

reformed character.

Of course Timmy told everyone of Meggie's

bravery, and when word got around she was

treated with a new respect by her peers. But,

although she didn't understand it, Meggie

knew it was the Stick, which was always

capitalized in her mind after that, that had

brought about the miracle. So she carefully

tucked it inside her book bag and carried it

everywhere she went, and if she needed help,

and who didn't at times? the Stick was always

there. She had privately christened it *No-See-Me* because it was a secret that nobody could see but her, and she never ceased to be amazed at the accuracy of the Stick's intuition. It was almost scary at times the way it seemed to know right from wrong, and guided her in the right direction, and she firmly believed it had intervened to help her mother.

CHAPTER TWO

Her mother was a pretty oval-faced woman with a good figure and a sweet generous smile, but in repose her face often looked pinched and helpless. Especially when her husband and Meggie's father, Jack Dawson, cheated on her, which he did on a regular basis. Jack was extraordinarily handsome with jet black hair, that he wore a bit long, and laughing green eyes. His smile was charming and somehow wistful, and when he engaged you in conversation you had the feeling that he thought you were the most important person on earth. Of course it didn't take Meggie long to discover that her dad gave everyone that impression, and she caught on to him at a very young age.

Which isn't to say that she didn't love him, or didn't enjoy being in his company.

Everything took on a special brightness when he was around, and he made every moment she was with him a big adventure. He took her places and bought her things her mom said they couldn't afford, and he had no scruples about charging them to her mom's account. And when the bills came in and there was no money to pay them, and things had to be returned, there were always tears and promises to do better. But he never changed his extravagant ways, and he never stopped loving the ladies.

"I don't think Jack's ever seen a pretty face whose owner he didn't want to bed," Meggie heard her mom telling her friend, LaVern, one day. She put up with his infidelities for quite a while, but finally couldn't take it any longer and divorced him. And Jack was saddened, shocked.

"Oh, Christ!" he said. "You don't mean that, Sally. I'll change."

Mom smiled sadly. "When pigs fly, Jack— as my dad used to say."

It was hard being completely on her own, but Mom made the best of it, and squaring her shoulders carried on. Until she started having trouble with her teeth. She was in a lot of pain and should have gone to the dentist right away, but because money was so tight she kept putting it off.

"Guess I can survive a little longer," she told Meggie, as she clutched her jaw. "Oh, God—if only your dad would send this month's check on time."

Meggie knew that was wishful thinking since her dad was already three months late with his child support payments and had a new girl friend, Maribelle, to boot. Maribelle was a nineteen-year old blond, whose clothes were a little too tight and who had a way of wiggling her hips when she walked, and although Meggie was annoyed with her dad for letting her mom down again, she secretly liked Maribelle. The girl was giggly and fun and always coming up with new ideas.

"Hey, Jack-o," she said one day when Meggie's dad had gotten a sales commission he hadn't expected and had picked Meggie up after school to celebrate. "Instead of splurging at MacDonald's, big spender, why don't you take me and the kid here to Disneyland with all that dough?" She poked Meggie in the ribs. "That sound good to you, honey?"

Did it ever! She'd been dying to see the Magic Kingdom and Cinderella's castle ever since her favorite homeroom teacher, Mrs. Collins, had invited several of the girls in her class to accompany her to Orlando during spring vacation. Mrs. Collins said she'd drive everyone there in her new station wagon and they could bunk at her brother's, who lived there. But the girls would have to pay for admission to the park every day and buy their own meals, and when Meggie heard that she knew it was impossible. Her mom had recently gotten a new job, a better paying job as assistant to the boss in a law firm downtown, and she was very happy about it. The boss' name was Clive Hawkins, and he was a widower with an eleven-year-old son, and he was strictly business in every way, she told

Meggie. He was the kind of man who kept his nose to the grindstone and didn't go in for any hanky-panky, that she'd had to put up with from previous employers. She was hopeful, and felt certain this time things would work out. But there were still old bills to pay. And her teeth, neglected so long, still had to be fixed. But Dad seemed to like Maribelle's suggestion.

"Not a bad idea," he said. And turning to Meggie, with one of his gorgeous smiles, he added, "So-o—is old Disneyland in the cards for us this year, baby-doll?"

Golly gee, I hope so! Meggie thought, thrilled to her toes. But almost unconsciously she opened her book bag and touched the magic Stick, and it immediately began moving in her hands. It started jumping up and down at a furious rate, vibrations coursing through her, and before she knew it she heard herself saying, "I'd like nothing better than going to Disneyland with you and Maribelle, Dad. But Mom's having a tough time right now, you know, making ends meet, and it just occurred to me that if you'd take the money you'd spend on my airline ticket and stuff we'd buy there, and give it to Mom—since you're already a bit late with the check—it might be better for all concerned."

"What?" Her dad flushed and looked embarrassed, especially in front of Maribelle. But he recovered quickly and blustered, "Well, okay, sweetie, if that's the way you feel. So be it."

And no more was said about Disneyland. But a few days later Mom got her check, and an extra hundred dollars as a bonus for the check being late. "Miracle of miracles!" Meggie heard her telling her friend, LaVern.

"I don't know how it happened, but I'm not going to look a gift horse in the mouth."

But Meggie knew how it had happened. She firmly believed that the Stick had pointed her in the right direction, telling her what she should do. And although it was a disappointment not seeing Disneyland when Mom cashed Dad's check and happily made her dental appointment at long last, the look of relief on her face was payment enough for Meggie.

The dentist said they'd start with a root canal and go on from there, and Mom, who'd waited so long, was actually looking forward to it. But one morning she awoke with an abscess on a back tooth and in terrible pain. She had been working overtime on a brief for her boss, bringing work home from the office and laboring far into the night, and she'd finally finished—when disaster struck!

"Oh, dear," she said to Meggie. "Now what am I going to do? I promised Mr. Hawkins I'd have this on his desk by ten today, and what's he going to think of me when I let him down? He seems like a very nice man, considerate, but I have a hunch he has no patience with people who renege on their promises. So call LaVern for me, will you, honey? and explain the situation. Ask her to take the brief over for me; she won't mind."

And Meggie was certain LaVern wouldn't have minded, good friend that she was, but when she called her there was no answer. She tried calling several times but no one picked up the phone, and finally, in desperation, she decided to take the brief to Mr. Hawkins herself. She knew from things her mom had said that her new boss was a stickler for punctuality and she didn't want her to get in trouble for not delivering what she'd promised on time. She knew the address of the Hawkins' law office, but not how to get there on the bus and decided she'd have to take a taxi.

She knew taxis were expensive, and she had no money, but her mom kept a jar in the cupboard, behind the cereal boxes, with any loose cash she had—her rainy-day fund, the called it. And when Meggie went to the cupboard and opened the jar on this day, hoping for the best, she found two dollars in bills and eighty-three cents in change. Was that enough? She had no idea. But picking up the phone she called a taxi.

Fortunately the taxi driver, a dark complexioned man with small laugh lines on each side of his mouth, was kind and understanding. When she told him the nature of her predicament and just how much money she had, he turned off the meter and said two bucks would be fine.

"Oh, thank you," Meggie said. "And you can have the eighty-three cents as a tip," she added generously.

She realized then that she'd have to borrow the money for the ride home from someone in her mom's office, but she didn't think that would be a problem. Her mom had said that everyone there was nice.

But when she stepped off the elevator at the Hawkins' law office, which was in an imposing building in the business section downtown, she was a little intimidated by the woman sitting behind the desk. She was a middle-aged woman in a dark suit with carefully coiffed auburn hair and looked pleasant enough, but she seemed to exude a no-nonsense air. "What do you want, little girl?" she asked Meggie. "This ia a law office. You lost or something?"

Meggie said, "No, I don't think so." And, taking a deep breath, she went on to explain that she was Sally Dawson's daughter and had a very important brief for Mr. Hawkins that she was delivery for her mother.

"And your mother sent you as her messenger?" the woman said, raising an eyebrow. "Well, whatever you've got hand it over; guess it takes all kinds."

She stuck out her hand, and obediently Meggie opened her book bag to get the brief and touched the Stick—which immediately began vibrating in her hand. She felt by now the familiar tremor coursing all through her, and heard herself saying, "Thanks, but I'd like to give the brief to Mr. Hawkins myself, if you don't mind."

"What? Don't be ridiculous! Give me that brief," the woman ordered.

But Meggie held her ground. She kept insisting she wanted to give the brief to Mr. Hawkins personally, and there followed a rather lengthy argument, until the door to the inner office opened and a man came out. He was a big, broad-shouldered man with a shock of dark hair, peppered with gray, and kindly, humor-filled eyes.

"Well, hello, who have we here?" he said smiling, and the woman behind the desk quickly explained the situation.

"She says she's Mrs. Dawson's daughter, Mr. Hawkins, and her mother sent her over with a brief for you," she told him, the expression on her face saying much plainer than words what she thought of a woman who'd do such a thing.

But to Meggie's relief Mr. Hawkins himself didn't seem fazed. "Interesting," he said. "To my knowledge Mrs. Dawson's never been late arriving in the short time she's been here. Did something happen today to delay her so that she had to send you?" he asked Meggie.

"You might say so, yes," Meggie told him. "My mom woke up with a terrible toothache this morning, because she's been putting off getting her teeth fixed, and simply had to go to the dentist."

"Really? That doesn't sound like Mrs. Dawson. Why did she wait so long I wonder?"

"She didn't have the money," Meggie said. Then quickly added, not wanting him to get the wrong idea, "It had nothing to do with her salary; she's very happy with what you pay her, sir. But my dad—well, he's a nice guy, but he's always late with his child support payments, and he left Mom saddled with a lot of debts she has to pay, you see. So she put off the dentist as long as she could—"

"You mean your mother's divorced? I had no idea," Mr. Hawkins said. "She seems so confident, the kind of person who has everything under control."

"Oh, she does, most of the time," Meggie assured him. "When this happened this morning, and the pain got so bad she couldn't stand it, she told me to call her friend, LaVern, and ask her to deliver the brief. And I tried to call LaVern three times, but she's not home I guess. Anyway there was no answer."

"So you decided to bring the brief over yourself, clear across town? What a brave girl you are."

"Well, I knew how important it was. Mom loves working here, and she didn't want to disappoint you, Mr. Hawkins. She admires the way you do things, how you run your office."

"And I admire her," he said. "I've noticed how hard working and diligent she is. Its impressed me. You should be very proud of your mother."

"I am," Meggie said. "And she'll be so glad you understood." Smiling she handed him the brief. Then screwing up her courage she asked if she could borrow the money for the taxi ride home. "Mom will pay you back right away, and I'd certainly appreciate it."

"Well, I think that could be arranged," Mr. Hawkins said. Suddenly he looked at his watch and exclaimed, "What do you know? It's almost lunch time. Would you give me the pleasure of having lunch with me? What's your name by the way, and is there any place special you have a hankering for?"

"My name's Meggie," she said, running her tongue over her suddenly dry lips. "And I sort of like McDonald's."

"So do I. McDonald's is fine. But there's a new place in town that's supposed to be pretty good. What do you say we try it?" And after giving the brief to the receptionist, he took Meggie's arm and led her down in the elevator to his car parked in the underground garage, and they went to a restaurant that was out of this world.

It was a lovely bright place on a lake with long glass windows opening onto a wide stone terrace filled with flowers and a magnificent view of the water. Meggie could hear soft music in the background and the waiters all wore white gloves, but the menu was a bit formidable. In addition to English it seemed filled with foreign words, French? she wondered, that she couldn't fathom. But Mr. Hawkins took care of that.

"May I order for you?" he asked.

"Please do." she said, relieved.

He ordered veal Florentine for the two of them and an interesting salad with avocado and nuts and a yummy chocolate soufflé for dessert. "That was one of the best meals I ever had," Meggie said, licking her spoon to get the last delicious morsel. "My mom would love this place, I bet."

"Maybe she'll come here sometime."

"Oh, I doubt it," Meggie said. "Someone would have to ask her and most of our friends aren't very rich. But I'll tell her about it, and I can't thank you enough for treating me."

"It was my pleasure," Mr. Hawkins said.

He drove her home then, and they arrived just as Mom pulled into the driveway. Her face was a little swollen, but she looked very pretty. She was wearing tight white jeans and a red sweater that showed off her slender figure to perfection, but she was startled to see Meggie with Mr. Hawkins. Meggie quickly explained how she'd tried and failed to contact LaVern and knowing how important the brief was decided to call a taxi and take it over herself.

"Which was certainly enterprising of her in my opinion," Mr. Hawkins said, with a broad smile. "I can't tell you how grateful I was. You have an exceptional daughter, Mrs. Dawson."

"Thank you. I think so," Mom said, as two splotches of red began to spread across her cheekbones. To be polite she asked him if he'd like to come in for a minute, and he said he'd like that very much. So they went inside and Meggie told her mother of the wonderful lunch they'd had.

"That was very kind of you to be so nice to my little girl, Mr. Hawkins," Mom said.

"Clive." He smiled again. "Please call me Clive. And, as I told Meggie, it was my pleasure, Mrs. Dawson."

'Sally. You can call me Sally, if you like."

"Thank you. I'd like that very much, Sally," he said. "We went to that new place, *Sans Souci,* that just opened. I thought it was excellent. Meggie thought you might like it too. I was wondering if you'd consider letting me take you there sometime."

"Why, yes, certainly," Mom said. And the red in her cheeks began to spread down her throat and onto her chest. "I'd like that very much, Clive."

"I'm glad, Sally," he said.

They were married six months later.

CHAPTER THREE

They went to Paris on their honeymoon
and had a wonderful time, shopping on
the Champs Elysées and dining in lots of
fabulous restaurants. Mom seemed happy
and content when they returned, and Uncle
Clive, as Mom said Meggie was now to call

Mr. Hawkins, was smiling, as if all was right with the world. They picked up Meggie at LaVern's, where she'd been staying while they were gone, and drove to Uncle Clive's house in West Hartford, a big white house with a nice yard filled with trees and flowers. They went inside and Uncle Clive called, "Josh? Where are you, boy?"

"In my room," a voice said. And they went upstairs to meet Uncle Clive's son, who'd been staying with his grandparents for several months.

"He's not a bad kid," Meggie had heard Uncle Clive tell her mom. "Kind of loud and boisterous at times. And he doesn't always apply himself in school like he should. But his heart's in the right place. I think you and Meggie will like him."

And he was right about that. Meggie liked Josh Hawkins from the first time she saw him lying flat on the floor, wearing shorts and sneakers and doing push-ups as he counted between his teeth, "Seventy-two, seventy-three, seventy-four—" until he reached a hundred. And Uncle Clive said, "Okay, Superman, cut that out and say hello to your new family."

"Sure, Dad," the boy said. And he jumped up and turned around and she saw that he was a fine looking boy, tall and wiry, with shaggy brown hair and dark eyes that reminded her of a squirrel's, the way they flashed and danced and never seemed to stay still.

"How many of those can you do?" Meggie asked, after the introductions had been made.

"Oh, a thousand, on a good day," he said airily. "Say, would you like to go in the bathroom?"

"No, thanks. I went before we came here."

He laughed. "Oh, I didn't mean that. Usually 'bout this time I chin on the shower rail, and I thought, if you didn't have anything better to do, you might like to watch."

And, of course, Meggie couldn't refuse such an offer. Josh was nice that way and considerate and fun to be with, and he and his best friend,

Ben Brown, who lived right next door, took her around and introduced her to all their friends. They played a lot of card games, Monopoly and Crazy Eights and something weird called Rummikub, and Josh always won. Meggie suspected that Ben could have won sometimes if he hadn't deliberately held back so as to give her a chance, but Josh wasn't bothered by any such scruples. However, he told her she was getting better, which was music to her ears.

She yearned for his approval—instinct told her that she already had Ben's, in spades—and she'd do anything to look good in Josh's eyes. So she tried her best to keep up in everything they did. They went on long bike rides and hikes in Elizabeth Park. And although sometimes she was so tired she longed to sit down and rest a minute, she never complained or admitted it. They also swam in a nearby lake, although Mom couldn't understand why they didn't use the pool at the country club.

"Your Uncle Clive just joined the club so you and Josh would have a nice place to go to," she told Meggie, "and now you won't even use it. What's wrong with you anyway?"

"Nothing, Mom," Meggie assured her. "The country club pool is nice, like you say, and the kids I've met there seem pretty nice, too. But you can't do anything much in that old pool. Just swim up and down, back and forth; you know? And that gets kind of boring after a while. But at the lake now there're lots of places to explore, and you see new things all the time."

"Well, just be careful," Mom said, a little frown puckering her forehead. "I know there's a lifeguard there, so I suppose it's safe enough. But don't let those boys get you into trouble. They're older and might want you to try things you're just not up to yet."

"Don't worry. I'll be careful," Meggie promised. And she kept that promise, after a fashion. However, instead of just wading into the lake with Ben, when she saw Josh crawling out on a tree branch one day, then swinging out over the water with all the grace of a circus acrobat, before letting go and dropping down with a wild whoop into the water, she said to Ben, "That looks like fun. Let's try it, whatta you say?"

"Oh, I don't know," Ben said, with a concerned look. "You could hurt yourself, Meg."

"Oh, poo!" she cried. And she scrambled out on a nearby branch before she could lose her nerve. Looking down— that water sure seemed a long way off, and butterflies started dancing in her stomach— but she ignored them. Letting go of the branch she swung out, as Josh had done, and, a few seconds later, landed in the water with a resounding plop.

"Atta girl!" Josh grinned, when she came sputtering to the surface. And that more than made up for the pain she was feeling, since she'd twisted her ankle when she hit the water at a wrong angle.

Sometimes she'd make sandwiches, peanut butter and jelly, or peanut butter and banana, Josh's favorite, and they'd have a picnic after their swim. They'd stretch out on the grass and talk about what they might do when they grew up. Ben said he'd like to be a teacher, or a guidance counselor maybe, and help kids with problems. And Josh said he couldn't make up his mind what he wanted to do exactly, there were so many exciting possibilities out there, like being an astronaut, or a deep-sea diver maybe.

"But how 'bout you, Meg?" he asked her one day, a gorgeous day with the sun shining brilliantly in a bright blue sky. There had been rain clouds in the morning that had threatened their picnic, but by noon when they started out there was a sudden rift in the heavy clouds that brought clear skies and everything was perfect. "You got any ideas about what you want to be when you're grown?" he added. "Besides being rich and famous, of course."

"Yep," Meggie said, without a moment's hesitation. "I want to be an author and write novels."

"Yeah?" Josh said, and she thought he looked a bit skeptical.

But Ben said, with an encouraging smile, "Why that's really great, Meggie. What kind of novels are you going to write?"

"Oh, I don't know." She shrugged. "I'm working on a novel right now about a South Pacific princess named Tahouri—"

"Who lives on an island due north of Tahiti," Josh said instantly, taking it up. "And I bet she likes to do the hula and is in love with a handsome prince—"

"How'd you guess?" Meggie smiled. "The prince's name is Ojeni, and his dad is the chief of the Origani tribe. Tahouri wants to get married and have lots of babies to populate the tribe, which has lost lots of warriors, due to war and stuff. But Ojeni isn't ready to settle down just yet, so what's poor Tahouri to do?"

"Maybe she'll find some way to convince Ojeni of all he's missing by holding off," Ben said. "Then he'll change his mind and waltz her to the alter, quicko."

"Or maybe the poor guy will recognize the grave danger he's in and hustle off to another island— or even another princess, before it's too late," Josh said, with a grin.

"Oh, you!" Meggie giggled, wrinkling her nose at him. And she lay back in the grass and watched the clouds drifting over the lovely sky and thought how lucky she was to have a big brother like Josh, who was smart and savvy and seemed to like having her around, and a good friend like Ben, whom you could depend on. And she was so grateful for all this good luck she tried her best to keep up in everything they did. But try as she might she sometimes felt she fell short in Josh's estimation. Like her failure at the Food Pantry, for instance.

The local Episcopal church which Mom and Meggie belongd to—Josh and his dad were Roman Catholics—sponsored the Food Pantry, which served meals to the poor and homeless. Mom sometimes volunteered there and one particular Sunday, a chilly, wintry day, she decided to take Josh and Meggie along to help.

"Listen, you scallywags," she said, with a pretend frown, "you're not doing anything, so get off your fannies and come with me. You might enjoy it, and it'll do you good to see how the other half lives."

So, somewhat reluctantly, they turned off the TV and went with her to the Food Pantry where they spent a couple of hours setting tables and washing dishes, while Mom and the other grown-ups ladled out the food. They fed over eighty-five people that day, Meggie was told, and she thought it was neat, but her feet hurt and she was glad when it was time to go home.

Only then they couldn't find Josh. He seemed to have disappeared. They found him finally huddled in a corner next to a bent-over old man with straggly hair and rheumy eyes. "What were you talking about with that person?" Mom asked him.

"I wasn't talking," Josh said. "I was listening. He was telling me how he lost his job, then his wife left him, and he started forgetting things. And now he's sleeping under the bridge; can you believe it?"

"Sad," Mom said, shaking her head. "You hear lots of sad stories in this place unfortunately. But there's not much we can do about it, honey. Except give them a meal and a warm place to come into out of the cold."

But obviously Josh didn't agree. He was always going to the Food Pantry after that by himself, doing what he could and, more important, listening to the peoples' stories.

He tried to get Meggie to go with him and to please him she did her best, but her heart wasn't in it. "I don't mind setting tables, or dishing out the grub," she said. "But then they always want to talk, and I don't know what to say to them."

"You don't have to say anything," Josh told her. "All you have to do is listen."

But she had a couple of bad experiences, one in particular that really turned her off. It was with an older man in a frayed jacket and torn jeans, with an unshaven face and long gray hair pulled back in a ponytail.

"Whatcha got there, girlie?" he asked, when she handed him a cup of coffee, and he promptly pulled a flask from his pocket and poured a hefty shot into the cup. "There that's better," he said, smacking his lips after he took a drink. "Want a sip, bright eyes?" Reaching out he put his arm around her and tried to pull her close.

"Don't!" Meggie cried, startled, and she gave him a hefty shove which caused him to spill his drink all over himself.

"Holy-yyy shit!" he cried. "Now look what you done? You nuts or somethin'?"

But Meggie didn't answer. She fled!

She thought she had no choice. Yet, among other emotions, she felt a deep sense of shame that somehow she'd let Josh down, and her throat ached with defeat. "I'm sorry I was such a failure," she apologized.

But Josh just brushed it off. "Oh, don't worry about it. The Pantry's not for everyone." And impulsively he took her hand and putting it to his lips kissed the tips of her fingers, but she was determined to make it up to him somehow. So she started doing things to please him. Like making hot chocolate, which he loved, on Sunday mornings, then going to the door to get the papers and bringing the things up to his room. She'd crawl into bed beside him, and they'd sip the hot chocolate and he'd read the funnies to her, and they'd giggle and have a great time. This went on for quite a while, and Meggie assumed it might go on forever. But suddenly she was thirteen. And on one certain Sunday, without warning, everything changed.

She got up early that day and made the hot chocolate and got the papers at the front door, and went up to Josh's room, as always. "Hey, lazy-bones, you gonna sleep all day?" she scoffed. And she went over to the bed and put the hot chocolate and her book bag, with the papers in it, on the bedside table. Then pulling back the covers she crawled into bed beside him and poked him in the ribs. But instead of laughing, as he usually did, he opened his eyes and glared at her.

"What you doing in here, brat?" he said grumpily. "Get lost."

"What? I've got the funnies. Don't you want to know what's happening in Peanuts?"

"No," he said. "I couldn't care less." And he jerked up to a sitting position and pushed her away. "Listen, you're not a little kid any longer. You're a teenager now, and you can't keep crawling into mens' beds, willy-nilly."

"I don't crawl into anyone's bed but yours."

"Yeah? Well, its gotta stop. I don't want you coming in here anymore; get it?"

"But why?" she said puzzled. "What's gotten into you, Josh Hawkins?"

"Nothing's gotten into me. I just think it's time you grew up, acted your age. You're so dumb you don't even know what you look like. And a lot of guys—well, I'm just telling you to be careful, that's all. You can't go around flaunting yourself like you don't have a care in the world."

Flaunting myself? "Are you nuts or something?" she said. "I don't know what you're talking about." And she was all set to start arguing with him, telling him how silly he was, when suddenly she had an insane desire to blow her nose. Reaching out she opened her book bag to get a tissue and inadvertently touched the Stick, which immediately began vibrating and the familiar tremor started coursing through her body. Then she heard herself saying, in a voice that didn't sound like her voice at all, "But on second thought, that's okay. Don't worry about it." And she jumped up from the bed and, gathering her things, started across the floor.

His windows were open and she could hear a chickadee buzzing in a tree, and she was determined not to let him see how hurt she was. But as she reached the door something made her turn and glance back, and what she saw was so startling her heart almost stopped beating. For Josh was crying, silently, his shoulders shaking up and down. And tears were streaming down his cheeks.

The next year he left for Brown, where he'd won a full four-year scholarship, and while he was gone she saw a lot more of Ben Brown. Ben was going to Trinity, right there in Hartford, so he was around a lot, and he took her to the movies and to parties at his fraternity house. He was always telling her how nice she looked and giving her compliments. "You have the brightest eyes I've ever seen. A man could drown in those eyes."

Meggie laughed. "I doubt that. But thanks anyway." And suddenly, for no reason, she was remembering the first time she tried to put on mascara. And Josh, who was watching, said, "Meggie, girl, you don't need that stuff.

Your eyes are fine just the way they are. They remind me of sunshine glimpsed through very clear water."

"Why, Josh, what a sweet thing to say." She was touched, for he was usually pretty stingy with his compliments. But then he had to go and ruin it all.

"It's probably just a matter of pigmentation," he said. "The color I mean." And then. as if embarrassed, he dropped his own eyes, the dark lashes making a shadow on his cheeks.

She thought it was funny, and kind of pathetic, how she remembered things like that.

Then Josh graduated from college, Phi Beta Kappa, and got a great job in a high-powered investment firm in New York. And Mom and Uncle Clive were so proud of him. "I knew he had it in him," Mom said. "I'm not at all surprised at his success."

And Uncle Clive laughed and said he expected Josh would be a millionaire before he was thirty. But Josh didn't let any of the accolades go to his head. He still came home on week-ends, and sometimes he took Meggie out, if she hadn't already promised to go somewhere with Ben.

"What's with you two?" he asked her one night, his mouth curved in a somewhat mocking smile. "You're not falling for good old Ben; are you, sweetheart?"

"Well, aren't you the crazy one," she said. And she told Ben just how annoying Josh could be at times, and he said that was just his way. "Don't listen to your brother," he advised her.

"How many times do I have to tell you, he's not *really* my brother," she said, somewhat crossly. "I mean we're no blood relation, which you know perfectly well. And I wish you'd stop calling him my brother. Do you do that just to annoy me?"

"Nope," he said. "But when he's your brother he's no competition."

CHAPTER FOUR

She was dumbfounded at that remark, and didn't know what to say. She still remembered how growing up she'd loved having a big brother like Josh, and was proud to be known as his sister. She had always liked him, enjoyed being in his company. But lately, and to her own surprise, that 'liking' had turned

to something else, although she was afraid

to put a name on it exactly. Yet every time

she looked at him her mouth went strangely

dry, and she got a funny, quivering feeling

in the pit of her stomach. What in God's

name was wrong with her? she wondered,

and she tried to forget it, put it behind her.

But every moment that she wasn't with him

seemed strangely dull and empty, and she

could think of no one but him. His looks,

his walk, his manner of speaking played over

and over in her mind until she thought she'd

go crazy. She wanted to touch him, put her arms around him in the worst way, just to see how it would feel. She never did, of course, but she wanted to so badly it was like an ache inside her.

In the meantime she enrolled at Middlebury College in Vermont because she heard it had a good English department, and she still dreamed of being a writer. And one day, almost as a lark, because she couldn't think of a subject to write about for an English assignment, she wrote a short story about

No-See-Me and the Amazing Crimson Stick. Of course she didn't write of her own experiences with the Stick, which had intervened on her behalf so many times and pointed her in the right direction. That was a secret she'd never told anyone, perhaps afraid they'd laugh, since she realized most people didn't believe in magic. But personally she'd always believed in fairy tales, and she had no trouble inventing a character with a problem for her English assignment, which the Stick solved pretty easily, naturally.

She didn't expect much from the little story. In her opinion it wasn't her best writing by any means, but to her surprise she got an A-plus for her effort. "This is excellent!" Professor Bradshaw, who was known as a very strict marker, wrote in the margin. "It's imaginative and very original. You're to be congratulated, Miss Dawson."

She couldn't believe it. But she was so happy she told Ben about it the next week-end she went home and gave him the story to read. And he liked it, too. He said it was great and asked if he could send it to his aunt, who was an editor at Scholastic.

She said, "Sure," and thought no more about it. By now she'd written a couple of dozen romantic stories and had sent them out to various magazines, but so far had gotten only rejections.

"Why is it nothing ever turns out like you want it to?" she complained to Josh one Saturday, when they were both home for the week-end.

"Who knows?" He shrugged. And he went on to say that he liked his job pretty well, but it was not as satisfying as he thought it would be. So he did other things to interest himself, and he kept talking about someone named Monica. It was always 'Monica this', and 'Monica that', and she got a little sick of hearing the name, to be honest.

"Say, boy, what's with this Monica?" she asked him jokingly one day, trying to ignore the twinge of jealousy she felt. "Is she pretty?"

"Pretty?" He looked absolutely baffled for a moment. Then he said, "No, she's not pretty, she's not pretty at all. Actually she's quite plain. But there's something about her, a kind of radiance. It shines through in everything she does."

"Are you in love with her?"

"In love with Monica?" He drew back as if she'd struck him. Then he said, almost vehemently, "Don't be ridiculous! It's hard to love a saint. They're hideously uncomfortable people to be around lots of times, because they're so good, you know, and they expect so much from you. You feel like such a failure, a nonentity, if you let them down."

"So you're saying this Monica is a saint?" Meggie said bewildered.

He nodded. "In every sense of the word. In her previous life she managed one of the most successful hedge funds on Wall Street, and pulled down a salary of over a million dollars a year. She lived in a Park Avenue penthouse and had a big place in the Hamptons, and she gave it all up without a backward glance."

"Why?"

"God called," he said simply. "And she didn't hesitate a moment. Now she's a nun."

"A nun? Where'd you meet her, for heaven's sake?"

"Through the Christophers. It's an organization that helps people. Monica runs a clinic for drug addicts on the Lower East Side. I help her out there sometimes, to give me something to do. If you'd like to meet her I could take you there sometime when you're home from school. You might enjoy it; whatta you think?"

"Okay," she said, a bit reluctantly. She didn't have any particular desire to meet this Monica, if the truth were known, but she was a bit curious, Josh talked about her so much. So the next Saturday she was home she took a train into the city and met Josh, and he took her to the clinic on the Lower East Side. And she finally met the sainted Monica, who was not at all what she expected.

In the first place she didn't look anything like a nun, or at least not the way nuns used to look, Meggie thought. Instead of wearing a habit, she was dressed in a pair of baggy coveralls, that didn't look too clean, and a gray sweatshirt, with the sleeves rolled up. She was tall and skinny and didn't have much of a figure, although you couldn't really tell since the coveralls covered her up pretty well. And she was quite plain, as Josh had said, with a rather long face and pale blue eyes, bordered by colorless lashes, and short, cropped salt-and-pepper hair. But she did have a warm, lovely voice and an all-encompassing smile that immediately put you at ease and made you feel welcome.

"So you're Josh's sister," she said to Meggie, when Josh went off to talk to someone. "He's told me so much about you."

"Really?" Meggie said. "All good I hope." And then something made her add, "He's not really my brother."

"Oh?" Monica looked puzzled.

"What I mean is, he's just my step-brother; we're no blood relation," she explained, a little too quickly, at the same time wondering why she'd brought that up. And Monica seemed to wonder, too.

'Oh?' she said again. "And you'd prefer it that way, that you're not actually related, I take it? So it can be just a man-woman, or boy-girl relationship, with the two of you?"

How intuitive she was. "Perhaps," Meggie said blushing. "Anything wrong with that?"

"Not at all," Monica assured her. "But I hope you realize, my dear, that our Josh marches to a different drummer. He's not your usual young man, with ordinary hopes and aspirations. He's searching for something else—I don't think he knows himself what it is exactly. But if I were you I wouldn't expect too much. I'd hate to see you get hurt."

"I don't think there's much danger of that," Meggie said, feeling slightly miffed for some reason. The nerve of this Monica! What did she know anyway?

Then Josh came back and took her around to meet some of the clients, as they were called, that he'd gotten friendly with. He showed her where the supplies were kept, and suggested

that she make some sandwiches, which she

did, ham and cheese and various cold cuts,

and passed them out. And all the while, from

the sides of her eyes, she was watching him as

he followed Monica around.

The clinic was really just one big room,

stark and spare, with a small kitchen space in

back and an office for the visiting doctor, who

showed up from time to time, Josh said. The

place didn't have much to recommend it, and

yet it seemed like a warm, friendly spot, thanks

to Monica, who never seemed to sit still. If she wasn't dispensing pills, or scheduling a dental appointment for someone, or arranging for a social worker to make a home visit to see what could be done for a family, she was smiling and cajoling and bestowing lots of encouraging little pats, when she sensed a pat was needed. And the recipients all loved her, Meggie realized. Somehow she made everyone feel that they were special, someone with still lots to offer the world as soon as they kicked a few bad habits—and they *would* kick them in time, she implied. She went from person to person, always happy to listen and giving a friendly squeeze to the shoulder.

"Good work, John," Meggie heard her say to someone, when he told her he'd been clean for two months. "I'm *so-o* proud of you; I *knew* you could do it!"

And to a shaggy-haired fellow named Joe, "Congratulations on finding that job. That's really great!" she told him. (Even if the job was just sweeping leaves in the park.)

It was obvious to Meggie that Monica was utterly sincere in everything she said and did, and that she loved these people unstintingly and with her whole heart. And it was equally obvious that Josh was impressed and admired her tremendously.

"Well, what do you think?" he asked Meggie at the end of the day. "Was Monica all I said? Did you like her?"

"Yes, very much," Meggie said, without a moment's hesitation and completely forgetting her initial annoyance with her. "She's really nice and certainly does a lot of good in that clinic."

"You can say that again!" Josh said, with a smile. "I think it's incredible the work she does there and all that she accomplishes, in her quiet, unassuming way. She's the most admirable person I've ever met in my life. No doubt about that."

"Hmm-mm," Meggie murmured, wondering why a simple statement like that should make her so nervous.

Then things took a turn for the better when Ben's aunt bought several of her stories for Scholastic—at Ben's urging she'd sent in a few more for consideration—and paid her the unbelievable sum of five thousand dollars.

She immediately quit college, which was beginning to bore her, and rented a place at the shore, determined to write the Great American Novel—or at least give it a try. The place she rented wasn't much, just a living room-kitchen combination and one small bedroom. But it had a fine view of the water and she liked it. Her mom, of course, was understandably upset. First, that she'd left school without getting her degree, and now was leaving home, too.

"I don't understand you," Mom said, looking around Meggie's new abode. "Why in the world would you give up a perfectly nice home, where everything's provided for you, to live in this—well, forgive me, honey, but this—this shack?"

Meggie sighed. "I know it isn't much, but it'll serve my purpose just fine. I'm a writer,

Mom, or trying to be. And writers need peace and quiet."

But Mom wasn't buying. "Are you sure you didn't get this place so you could have someplace to be alone with Josh?"

"Why what an idea!" Meggie said. But she could feel herself blushing, and it was hard to meet her mother's eyes.

"Darling, don't go down that road," Mom warned. "I love Josh like my own; he's the son I never had. But in spite of his many fine qualities he's not for you, Meg. He'll break your heart if you let him, just like your father broke my heart. Which isn't to say that I didn't love Jack Dawson, or that I don't love him still with one part of me, if the truth were known. I have a wonderful marriage with Clive. He's truly a husband *extraordinaire,* financially, sexually, in every way."

"But he's not Jack," Meggie said. "Oh, Mom, don't you think I know that?" She still remembered how her mother used to look when Jack took her in his arms, the undisguised joy and spontaneity that seemed to suffuse her whole body. But she also remembered the look of utter misery on her face when Jack cheated on her. So she said, "Relax. Josh isn't like Daddy. It might sound corny, but in my opinion he's really true blue."

"I don't doubt it, sweetie. I'm sure his heart's in the right place. But that's the trouble, don't you see? As much as he might want to, he'll never give you all of himself because he's searching for something else. I don't know what it is; perhaps he doesn't know himself, but when he finds it he'll leave, and you'll be bereft. Don't count on Josh Hawkins to bring you happiness."

But, of course, she didn't listen to her mother. How could she, when what she felt for Josh was throbbing and growing to such an extent it was like a constant yearning pain inside her. So she bought a few things for the cottage and fixed it up a bit. Then she called Josh at work one day and invited him up for the weekend. She said it wasn't the Waldorf Astoria, but if he didn't mind roughing it a bit—and he laughed and said he was still a Boy Scout at heart. And on Friday night he arrived, bringing his old sleeping bag which he laid down on the living room floor.

And the next morning, after she got the paper and made coffee and saw he was awake, she asked him, "How'd you sleep?"

"Not too well," he admitted, pulling on his chin. "This old floor is pretty darn hard."

"I was afraid of that," she said. Then deciding it was now or never, she swallowed and said boldly, "You know I've got a perfectly good bed, very comfortable, in the next room, that I wouldn't mind sharing. You interested?"

He didn't answer for the longest moment. Then he grinned broadly and said, "Now that's an offer I can't refuse." And he got up from the floor and put his arms around her and kissed her, not the light feathery kisses or the pecks on the cheek that he'd given her in the past, but a real kiss that sent her pulses zinging. And he said not a word as he waltzed her straight into the bedroom, and they made love for the first time, and it was absolutely wonderful as she knew it would be. And Josh seemed to think so, too.

"You're so sweet," he told her, running his lips down her cheek. "You're positively the dearest, sweetest girl—the funniest, too. But I've always known that."

"Oh, Josh," she said, "I'm so happy." Her heart was almost exploding with happiness, and she couldn't imagine what she'd done to be so lucky. But she felt in her bones that this kind, wonderful guy would protect her and cherish her, always. And she thought it would go on forever; why not? They had such fun together, such wonderful times.

He bought an old beat-up canoe at a tag sale, and he'd take her canoeing in the bay, stopping somewhere along the shore that looked promising. She'd unpack the cooler with the lunch she'd prepared, the paninis and the marble cake that he loved, and they'd devour everything to the last crumb. And after they'd eaten their full they'd stretch out on the grass and he'd put his head in her lap, and she'd play with his hair as she gazed down at his face. Such a wonderful face, so handsome and alert; even in repose his face looked bright and alive. She'd smile at his eyelashes, those thick, dark lashes that curved upward in a long, sweeping arc and run her fingers down his nose and across his cheeks and to his lips, and she'd think of how much she loved him, and he loved her too. She was sure of that!

"You know, considering you're not bad looking, you're a great cook too," he said one day with a look of tender amusement. It was a perfect

June day, clear sky with just the hint of a breeze, and the sunshine coming through the trees was warm and golden and somehow mysterious.

She made a mock face. "So is that all I'm good for, cooking?"

"No," he said. "You've got a few other attributes I could mention if I tried." And reaching up he put his hands around her neck and pulled her face down to his.

She smiled, brows raised in anticipation, and she wasn't disappointed as his mouth found hers and almost crushed hers with its hard urgency. But she didn't care. She welcomed the thrill of what it promised, as he pulled her down beside him and turned her over, and they made love, she clutching his backside with both hands and opening her legs as far as they would go and raising her hips, all the while urging him to go faster and deeper, again and again, until they both came in a wild spurt of energy.

When it was over she sagged weakly against him, filled with a wonderful sense of dreamy satisfaction. And he seemed to feel the same way. "God!" he said. "You're really something, baby."

"And there's more where that came from."

He grinned "If you don't kill me first."

"Never," she giggled. "I want you around for a long time, Buster."

CHAPTER FIVE

And that's the way it was. They laughed and loved, and each time they came together it seemed better than the time before. Sometimes they'd fall quickly into bed, their hands and mouths frantic for each other, for each delight along the way, until they came, soaring swiftly to incredible heights. But at other times it was slow and easy, like the waves in an undulating sea, as they savored every moment. And every time was precious to Meggie. She didn't think she'd ever get enough of Josh, and she was certain he felt the same way.

Every morning he'd leave for his job in the city, and she'd concentrate on her novel, which had gone through many metamorphoses through the years. In the latest version she was working on Princess Tahouri, of her childhood fantasy, and her handsome prince,

Ojeni, had now become Margo Fontaine, a talented designer in a prominent New York fashion house, and Ojeni was known as Ronald Kittredge, an up-and-coming stock broker. They were both still attractive and delightful, and, of course, madly in love, but to feel totally complete Margo (Tahouri) wanted to get married and have babies. However, unfortunately Ronald (Ojeni) was still skittish about committing himself.

So what else is new? Meggie asked herself when the writing wasn't going very well, which it wasn't, and then she started running low on money. From the beginning Josh had insisted on paying his share of the expenses, and she was in no danger of losing the cottage. But she didn't like being so low on funds, and curious to see what would happen she wrote a few more *No-See-Me* stories and got herself an agent. And the agent sold them for more money than she'd gotten for the previous stories and, although she didn't know it at the time, a whole new career had opened for her. And life continued in this pleasant state.

Late in the afternoon Josh would come home, and they'd spend an hour or so in bed, as if their hunger for each other had only begun. Afterwards they might shower together, laughing like children as they soaped and sprayed, catching up on each other's day. It was almost as if they'd lived this way forever, and it was so perfect Meggie could see no reason why it shouldn't continue. They'd have a drink and cook dinner, Meggie introducing him to some new recipe she'd found in a magazine, and after dinner they'd often turn on the stereo and dance. She'd feel his hands moving over her, caressing the length of her back and molding her hips, and her whole body would feel sensual and alive as he pulled her tighter against him.

And it was strange how during all this time she felt a peacefulness, a confidence that she had never known before. Sometimes she'd look up at him, as if to be sure he was really there, and he'd smile at her, or reach out and touch her hair or squeeze her hand, as if to reassure her. And later when they climbed into bed and made love, she'd fall asleep with his arms wrapped securely around her. She loved everything about their life together and prayed it would never end. His gentle camaraderie, his subtle wit enchanted her, and she enjoyed the lively sparring they engaged in as much as he did. She thought later that it was just a fool's paradise, and she should have known that it was too good to last—but at the time it seemed heaven personified.

"I feel so fortunate," she confessed one day, hugging her arms. "Sometimes I want to pinch myself, wondering what I did to deserve such happiness." It was a chilly Saturday morning at the beginning of the month, and the first snap of fall was in the air, after a spell of Indian summer. Bright fall leaves of red and gold decorated the landscape and Josh was enjoying his second cup of coffee on the deck.

"Well, I wouldn't worry about it," he grinned, and she saw the amusement in his eyes. "You're just darn lucky I came along when I did. Just think, if it hadn't been for me, and all my manly charms, you might have ended up a dried-up old maid. You're so homely, so downright hard on the eyes—"

"Oh, you!" she said, swatting him. And she jumped in his lap, almost causing him to spill his cup of coffee.

"Hey, watch it," he cried.

But she took the cup from him and placed it on the railing. "Well, I certainly hope our kids don't inherit that mean streak of yours," she said, in a voice of mock seriousness.

"Our kids?" he repeated, and he looked suddenly perplexed, for she'd never mentioned children before. "Tell me, do you spend a lot of time thinking about kids, the future, the whole marriage bit?"

"No," she said, "not much time; actually hardly any time at all." Which was a bald-faced lie, of course. For she did spend untold hours thinking of their marriage and the babies she hoped to have with him someday. She often dreamed of little girls with dimpled cheeks and bouncing dark curls and small boys with irrepressible grins, and at such times she felt very close to her old friend, Princess Tahouri. But something told her that Josh wasn't ready for that yet, so she kept quiet, not wanting to scare him. And in a few moments she saw his face relax and he was smiling again. And they went back to the foolishness, which she reveled in, and she didn't have a care in the world.

Their time together was so perfect she didn't want anything to disturb it, and she worked hard to assure that nothing would. But then, for no reason, and out of the blue, she began to feel uneasy. It was nothing she could put her finger on exactly. But Josh seemed distracted on occasion, and she wondered what was wrong.

"Is something bothering you, darling?" she asked him one night, as they lingered over a late dinner. They were sitting on the deck as they often did, with their feet propped up on the railing, watching the moon popping over the horizon. Rainstorms had threatened the area all day with clouds dark and angry and flashes of lightning ripping the sky. But the rain had passed them by and the late August night was now calm and clear.

Josh denied there was anything bothering him. "Nope," he said. "Everything's hunky-dory." But she noticed his mouth tightening at the corners, and he seemed to have trouble meeting her eyes.

"Let's not have any secrets from each other. Please!" she implored him. "If I've done anything to upset you just tell me, and I'll do my best to change it. Okay?"

But he said she was imagining things. And jumping up he started clearing the table they'd eaten on, taking things inside to the sink. But inbetween his trips she saw a flush sweeping over his forehead and down his cheeks to his collar, and her heart did a funny flip. *What's he hiding?* a little voice inside her asked, and she was painfully aware suddenly that she was holding her breath.

But life went on. And there were moments, especially during those last few months, when his sweetness towards her was almost more than she could bear. One night when the moon was just beginning to come up, a thin slice of silver in the sky, they went for a long walk on the beach. They were chatting about nothing in particular when suddenly he stopped walking and leaning down took her face in his hands. And he said, with intensity, "Listen, Meggie, girl, you're everything a man could ever want in a woman. And don't you forget it."

"Oh, Josh," she said touched. "Oh, darling." Tears filled her eyes, and she was almost overcome with happiness.

But that night she awakened as from a nightmare, and feeling lost, completely disoriented, cried out, "Josh, oh, Josh—where are you?"

"Right here, sweetie," he said, and he put out his hand and touched her thigh beneath the nightgown, and soon, almost before she knew it, they were making love. And it was just as good as always, which gave her a measure of comfort and momentarily calmed the almost paralyzing sense of foreboding she felt. But the fear didn't go away, as much as she told herself there was nothing to worry about. And things went on that way all through the fall when the days began to shorten and there was the smell of wood smoke in the air.

Then Josh came home one night and announced, almost casually, that he'd quit his job, that wonderful job that Uncle Clive predicted would make him a millionaire before he was thirty. "But why?" Meggie asked, not so much shocked as bewildered. "I thought you really liked it there."

"Oh, I liked it well enough," he said. "But lately, I don't know, I kept asking myself what was I doing there? There must be more to life than the pursuit of the almighty dollar; don't you agree?"

"I suppose so," she said, although she wasn't exactly sure what she was agreeing to. "Anyway if you were unhappy there I'm sure you can find something else, something you'll like better without any trouble. That shouldn't be a problem, you're so smart."

"Think so?" He grinned wryly. "That's nice to hear, but I don't know about that *smart* bit. I feel pretty dumb at times. But I intend to look around, see what's out there."

And good as his word he did look around, sent out his resume to half-a-dozen places. He also went on a couple of interviews where he was actually offered a well-paying job. But nothing seemed to appeal to him. "They're just not what I want," he told Meggie, running a hand over his face. "Just more of the same-old, same-old; know what I mean?" He didn't seem overly concerned, however—but she noticed his hand, clenching and unclenching into a fist.

She sensed he was struggling to come to grips with something, and she had no idea what it was, but she tried hard to understand. Unfortunately, there wasn't much she could offer in the way of help, but reaching up she put her hands on his shoulders and laid her cheek against his chest. "Don't worry, honey," she whispered. "I'm sure things will work out for the best."

"Sure, they will," he said. But he didn't sound really convinced. And then because he had a lot of time on his hands and to give himself something to do, he told Meggie, he started spending time with Monica again at the clinic. But that didn't worry her at first because she didn't consider Monica a rival— after all she was a nun.

But as time went on, and he spent more and more time in Monica's company, she could feel him changing in a subtle way. The inertia and uncertainty he'd been displaying began to disappear, and he seemed filled with a new purpose, a new resolve.

Curious, she asked him one day, "Just what do you really do at the clinic?" And he smiled and said, "Oh, a lot of different things. I help Monica dispense the meds and listen as she talks to the clients. She needs all the help she can get. There're so many poor souls out there." He shook his head sadly, his brows knitted together in concern. "Did you notice that woman with the bandaged face, by any chance, the day you visited the clinic?"

"Yes," Meggie nodded. "I was wondering—was she in a car accident?"

"No. Her pimp knocked out her teeth and cut her face with a razor, when she tired of giving him all her money and tried to get away from him. Monica found her lying on the street in a pool of blood and took her to the ER. Then Monica found a dentist to give her new teeth, free of charge. And now she's located a plastic surgeon who's agreed to fix the poor gal's face, again for free, in a series of operations.

"And do you recall that good looking black kid with the big smile? He'd been sentenced to twenty-five years in the pen for robbing a bank. But Monica discovered he wasn't even there. He'd been forced to join this gang that did some really bad things, and the judge found him guilty by association. But after Monica visited him in jail and heard his story, she got him a new lawyer, who somehow finagled a new trial for him. This time he was found innocent of all charges, and now he's on probation for five years doing community service and other things. It would have been a death sentence for him if he'd gone to prison, with his looks."

"Amazing!" Meggie said, and she meant it. "Monica sounds like a real wonder woman."

"Yes. She's astounding; that's the only word for her," Josh said. And he continued working at the clinic and singing Monica's praises, and Meggie wondered why his doing something so admirable left her so nervous.

But she was still worried, and one night soon after that, as they were walking again on the beach beneath a glossy white moon, with insect choruses filling the air, she gathered up her courage and said, in a firm, clear voice, "I love you, Josh Hawkins. Whatever's going on inside you now, that I don't understand, I want you to remember that. Every hour, every morning, every night, for the rest of your life, remember—I love you!"

"And I love you," he said. But he seemed to hesitate before he said it, and she was suddenly so scared she felt sick to her stomach. Something dark began rising inside her, spreading out to her arms and legs, her fingers and toes, her head.

"Please! Don't shut me out," she begged him, as a certainty that something awful was going to happen swelled in her breast. "Whatever it is, we can work it out."

But he only sighed sadly and said, "Can we? I seriously doubt that, Meggie, sweet. There are some things a person can't ignore, as hard as he tries."

And the next day, while she was working on another *No-See-Me* story to send to her agent, he came up to where she was sitting at her desk and calmly told her that he was going to a seminary.

"A seminary? What's that? A place where you study to become a minister?"

"Or in my case, where you study to become a priest."

"A priest?" She stared at him wide-eyed, completely baffled. "You're thinking of becoming a priest? Since when?"

He smiled, a small, enigmatic smile. "I wish I could answer that, but I don't really know. I think I've always had this quest inside me, this hunger for something more. But I didn't know what it was until I met Monica, started helping her in the clinic. And suddenly, it was as though I'd finally found myself, my purpose in life—although I know that'll be hard for you to understand."

To put it mildly, she thought, her mind reeling. She could see the wide sweep of ocean outside the window and the clear blue of the sky, and her heart was thumping so loudly she thought he'd hear it.

"I'm such a coward," he was saying, "I've put off telling you, but it can't be avoided any longer. I've had this calling I can't ignore, so I'm leaving for a seminary in upstate New York this coming Monday. I don't want to hurt you, but believe me, I have to do this."

"No, you don't! Don't go!" she begged him. Then tossing pride to the wind she jumped up and grabbing his arms, looking into his face, pleaded, "Don't leave me, Josh! Please! I won't ask for much. You don't have to marry me, if you don't want to. I wouldn't expect anything that grand. But can't we go on like we've been doing? Can't you keep on loving me, just a little?"

"Ah, Meggie," he said, looking stricken, "you've got it all wrong. I could never stop loving you, not in a million years. I've always loved you, ever since we were kids. But I couldn't make you happy. This other thing would always come between us. I tried to forget it, but I can't. There's a calling inside me that draws me to the priesthood."

"Then why don't you join the Episcopal church?" she said, desperately. "Listen, Episcopal priests can get married, have childen, lead normal lives."

But he said simply, "I couldn't do that. I'm a Catholic. And I have to do this. I have no choice. It just happens sometimes."

"But what about me?" she asked, in a choked voice. She was numb with shock and tears were suddenly streaming down her cheeks. She felt as if the whole world had turned upside down in a single moment, and she was filled with despair. "We've been so happy together—at least I thought we were. Was it all just an act on your part?"

"No! Never!" he assured her. And he put out his hands in a helpless gesture that was so pathetic she had to close her eyes for a moment. "These last few months were truly wonderful," he said. "I'll never forget them— our time together. But I have to move on."

And then trying for a note of jollity to ease things perhaps, he added, in a light, teasing tone, "Anyway you shouldn't take it so hard, Meggie, darling. Why, heck, the minute I'm out of the picture you'll have more guys falling over you than you'll know what to do with."

"Oh, stop!" How could he joke about something that was tearing her apart? The thought of how much she would miss him, how much she missed him already, caused a sudden aching emptiness inside her. And suddenly a queer, shooting pain took over her chest and she wanted to scream, throw something, anything to relieve the pressure. Her legs felt so weak she thought she might fall, and she staggered back to her desk and plopped down, her hands automatically clutching the crimson Stick she'd been writing about. And immediately, as always, the familiar tremor started coursing through her body, and her nerves instantly stopped their jangling.

And she heard herself saying calmly, almost stoically, "Okay, if that's the way it has to be.

Do what you have to do, Josh. But I want you to remember one thing. I love you, and I'll always be here if you change your mind, want to come back. And that's a promise."

"Thanks," he said, obviously relieved that she was accepting the inevitable. "That's really kind of you, Meg—and I'll remember." Smiling he leaned over and gave her a quick hug. Then he was gone.

CHAPTER SIX

He left for the seminary then, and when he was ordained he joined the Jesuits and was sent to Africa. And he wrote Mom and Uncle Clive that he was happy, he was content for the first time in his life, he said—although it was a slightly different story with Meggie.

Later she often wondered how she got through that time, since she felt as though she had died inside, her heart, her soul, her mind. She could hardly breathe, the loneliness was so intense and the realization that she'd lost Josh, she'd very likely never see him again, hurt so much she thought she'd go mad from the pain. It was almost beyond bearing, and she might not have made it at all if it hadn't been for Ben.

Her mom and Uncle Clive were sympathetic, and Mom refrained from saying, "I told you so," but they didn't really understand what she was going through. It was Ben who came over every day after Josh left and just held her in his arms and let her cry. It was Ben who brought her food and insisted she take a few bites. It was Ben who took her to the circus and smiled when she laughed at the clowns.

And it was Ben who asked her to marry him, not once, but several times, although she always refused. "Thanks, but I can't marry you, guy," she said. "It's nice of you to offer, and I appreciate it. But it wouldn't be fair to you, considering I love someone else."

"Oh, I know," he said. "I know how you feel about Josh, although I wonder why sometimes—I mean considering."

"You and me both," she said sadly. "It's crazy—he doesn't want me."

"But I do!" Ben said. "I think we could have a good life together, Meggie. I wouldn't ask for very much, and maybe you'll get over Josh in time."

Never! I'll never get over Josh Hawkins! she thought. But she liked Ben. He had a sweet manner and his voice was always calm and pleasant. In all the years she had known him she had never heard his voice raised in anger. When he was really annoyed, and that was rare, he spoke slowly and deliberately, the nostrils of his nose distending just a little. He was thoughtful and sensitive, and there was a gentleness about him that drew little children and animals to him like a magnet. He also had a special kind of radar that seemed to sense when someone was unhappy or upset and tried to do something about it. All in all

he was a nice, warm, funny human being,

who did not have a mean bone in his body

and was the kind of friend you could depend

on. He was also smart and ambitious and

would probably go far in life. But he wasn't

Josh, and she didn't love him.

And then one night, when she was working

on another *No-See-Me* story, he dropped in

unexpectedly and asked her to marry him

again. Only this time he said it was different.

He said he'd finally seen the light, and if she refused he wouldn't ask her again.

Meggie smiled, because she'd heard that song before, and was prepared to once more say, "No." But then her hands touched the crimson Stick lying on her desk, and instead of "No", to her surprise, a resounding "Yes" popped out of her mouth.

"What?" Ben said startled. "Do you mean it, darling?" And he caught her to him in a great bear hug and kissed her soundly, before she could change her mind.

So they were married in a pretty ceremony in her mother's and Uncle Clive's back yard with all their friends present, wishing them the best. Ben was so happy he kept saying, to all and sundry, that he was the luckiest man alive, and Meggie played the part of the happy bride to perfection—although, if the truth were known, she felt completely empty inside.

And that night, their wedding night, as she lay in his arms thinking of Josh, Ben surprised her by saying, "I hope I didn't disappoint you, sweetheart."

"Oh, Ben, don't think such things. It was fine," she said guiltily. "Just fine."

"Well, I don't know about that. But it doesn't bother me that Josh was first."

"You're too good," she told him.

"No," he said, wiping the tears from her eyes. "I just hope that someday you'll forget about Josh and love me."

And she did love Ben, she thought now, as she stood in her bedroom, scanning the contents of her closet. They'd had twenty-five years together, and she couldn't have asked for a better, more understanding husband. But it hadn't all been smooth sailing, by any means. She'd had her share of trouble, of heartache, she thought, remembering Robin, their first child, a beautiful, golden-haired angel she had almost died giving birth to, which had made the little girl almost more precious to her. She hadn't realized it was possible to love anyone so much, her little face, her tiny hands, the way she depended on her mother for everything filled Meggie with delight.

But as sweet as Robin was she didn't completely fill the aching longing still inside her. And her marriage, for all its pluses, wasn't as satisfying as it could have been. Ben was the perfect husband in many ways, always kind and considerate, but the truth was she found him a bit boring. She felt she knew what he was going to say before he opened his mouth, and she yearned for a little variety, some excitement.

Then her mother, who'd just returned from a trip to the Holy Land, where she'd gone with her book club group and had broken her foot traversing Jerusalem's cobblestoned streets, asked her to chair the next meeting of the club, of which she was president.

"I could probably handle it," she said, "but this darn foot is still giving me a lot of trouble, and I don't want to stand on it anymore than I have to. So if you could take over the meeting for me, sweetie, I'd really appreciate it."

"Oh, I don't know—" Meggie said, hesitating. "What would I have to do exactly?"

"Nothing much. Just read the book, *The Lemon Tree*, that we've been studying, so you can discuss it. The book is an eye-opening account of Israeli-Palestinian relations and why the conflict remains unresolved."

"But isn't that mostly due to the fact that the Arabs aren't very co-operative?"

"I know, I know." Mom sighed. "Before I read the book I felt that way, too. I was all for Israel, no doubt about it. But now I'm more inclined to be pro-Palestinian. It was so sad the way those poor people were kicked out of their homes and dispersed to make room for the Israelis. That's why Professor Mandow says privately he doesn't think there will ever be any real peace between the two factions in our lifetime— the bitterness is so intense."

"Who's Professor Mandow?"

Mom smiled. "This perfectly fascinating man. He's a visiting professor at Inter-Faith Theological, you know that non-denominational graduate school for religious studies that offers masters and doctoral degrees. He's teaching a course there on the Middle East, and when I called the school to see if they knew of anyone who'd talk to our group, for a fee, of course, they suggested I contact Professor Mandow. So I called the number they gave me, and his assistant, Mouse, set everything up. She arranged for Marti, which he asked me to call him, to speak to us before we left for the Holy Land, and to meet with us again now that we're back. Mouse took care of everything"

"Mouse?" Meggie said, lifting an eyebrow.

Mom laughed. "I thought that name was a joke, too, when I first heard it, but it actually fits her very well. Mouse is a nondescript little woman who seems to be all gray—gray hair, gray eyes, gray complexion; even her clothes are drab, completely colorless. But she's very efficient. I'll give you her number, and if you call her she'll give you a time and date that's convenient for Marti to meet with our group again."

So, to please her mom, Meggie called the woman named Mouse, introduced herself, and told her of Mom's accident. Mouse said she was very sorry to hear of it and would inform the Professor and get back to her soon. And less than an hour later the Professor himself called and said he was shocked to learn of his good friend, Sally's, misfortune, and suggested he and Meggie meet for coffee to go over some of his notes. They met at an outdoor café near the school, and the minute she saw him Meggie felt she was in the presence of a most unusual individual.

He was a tall man, slim and lithe, with dark, curly hair getting gray and strong features in a tanned face. His eyes were dark, too, and narrowed, as if he'd spent a lot of time squinting into the sun, and there was a long, jagged scar running from his right eye across his cheek and down to his mouth, which cut his face nearly in half, but oddly didn't detract from his attractiveness.

He stood up from the table where he was seated as he saw her approaching and smiled, a smile so warm and welcoming it left her a little breathless.

"So you're Sally's daughter," he said. "I expected you to be pretty—but are you as nice as your mother?"

"Time will tell," Meggie said, and she laughed, a bit flustered, as he pulled out a chair for her and asked what she'd like to drink.

"Coffee would be fine," she said, sitting down. She told him she was half-way through the book, *The Lemon Tree*, and, like her mother, was beginning to identify more with the Palestinians than the Israelis. "It was so sad the way their land was just taken from them, and they were kicked out of their homes."

"Yes," he said. "I agree, very unfortunate. But you must remember the same thing happened to the Israelis."

"Really? When was that?"

"Two thousand years ago. The Israelis have been fighting for a homeland ever since the Romans destroyed them as a nation."

"Hm-mm," Meggie murmured, aware suddenly that she was out of her element.

And, as if realizing that, and to put her at ease, he changed the subject. "So—how'd your mother like the Holy Land?"

Meggie smiled. "She loved it. Mom said, even if you weren't particularly religious, you couldn't help feeling a bit closer to Christ when you walked on the same ground he'd walked on so long ago. Did you have that same feeling, Professor, by any chance?"

"That I felt closer to Christ? No." He shook his head. "But then I'm a Jew, and I don't feel the same about Christ as most Christians do."

"Oh," she said embarrassed, "I'm sorry. I didn't realize you were Jewish. Your name doesn't sound particularly Jewish to me. Is it Jewish?"

"No. My parents changed it. My real name is Asa Levanthal, and I'm a Bulgarian Jew. My parents fled Bulgaria to escape the Holocaust and settled in Israel. My parents were proud to be Jewish, or so they said, but they felt the name Levanthal might be a handicap for their children in the world at large, so they selected the innocuous Mandow, out of the blue. I don't particularly like it, but I'm used to it, and I'm a real Israeli, in spite of the name."

"How interesting," Meggie said. And as he opened his briefcase and shared his notes with her, from his last meeting with her mother's group, she began to see why Mom found him so appealing. There was an air of confidence and ease about him, as if he was completely happy in his own skin, and she relaxed and enjoyed being with him.

They discussed the agenda for the next meeting of the book club, and Meggie looked forward to what he'd say there. And she wasn't disappointed. "You did such a good job," she told him enthusiastically when they met for coffee again. "Most of the women in the club, my mom's friends, are really interested in Mid-Eastern affairs and want to learn all they can. I thought it was remarkable how you listened so politely to what they all had to say, and then pointed out the other side of the coin they weren't aware of."

"Thank you," he said, "but you're too kind. Those ladies were a very receptive audience and weren't likely to question anything I told them."

"Still, it was a great learning experience for them—and for my mom too. She's fascinated by that whole Arab-Israeli conflict and wants

to learn everything she can. And you helped

her a lot with your insights."

"You're too kind," he said again. And

reaching over he covered her hand, that was

lying on top of the table, with his and gave it

a gentle squeeze. "I have some other things in

my repertory that I'd be happy to share with

your mother," he said casually, "if you think

she'd be interested. Perhaps we could meet

again, you and I, and I could show you some

of the stuff I have in mind—various books, artifacts, and so on."

"That would be very nice of you," Meggie said. "But I don't know what my mother could do with it exactly."

"Oh, she could always write a paper. Say, 'A housewife's view of the conflict in the Holy Land.' Newspapers are always interested in human interest stories like that."

"They are? Well, that's certainly a possibility. I don't think Mom has ever considered writing a paper, but she might like seeing her name in print. And she's really interested in the subject."

"Great! So why don't you call Mouse—you have her number, right?—and she can give you a time that would be convenient for you to drop by my place to see the things."

"Okay," Meggie nodded. And that's the way it began. She had no intention of starting anything with this man, who was old enough to be her father. But he'd awakened a kind of curiosity inside her, and a strange lethargy seemed to have overtaken her senses. And when his assistant, Mouse, dropped by the house the next day and gave her a keycard to his room in a Hartford motel, and said the professor would expect her at seven that evening, she didn't even question it. She felt she had nothing better to do, so what the heck? and she showed up right on time—although he was half-an-hour late. But as soon as he arrived he started working his magic.

"Dear girl, let me look at you," he said. And he put his hands on her shoulders, then held her off from him a little, as he surveyed her from head to toe. "You know, you're really very beautiful," he said. "I don't think any man who'd ever had you could ever forget you."

"Thanks—but that's not true," Meggie said. "My first love, whom I adored, left me to fulfill a dream he had inside him."

"He'll be back."

"I doubt that."

"Well, I don't," he grinned, "not for a moment. I think you're quite irresistible, my dear. The kind of woman who gets in a man's blood and makes it impossible for him to get her out of his mind."

"Oh, please." She was embarrassed, and knew she was blushing. Yet at the same time, and to her surprise, she was aware of a strange fascination.

There was something about him, a charm, a kind of sheer animal magnetism that was hard to resist. "So what have you got to show me?" she asked, anxious to change the subject. Then added, half-jokingly, "Are you going to make it worth my while, my coming over here, Professor?"

"I'll let you be the judge of that." He laughed, and releasing her shoulders slipped an arm about her waist and led her over to a table near the window. There were several books there on display— *A History of the Arab-Israeli Conflict, The Question of Palestine, 1948, A History of the first Arab-Israeli War,* to name a few. There were also pages from Hebrew prayer books that had been damaged during the Holocaust and ancient Jewish papyri dating to the 5th century BC, he pointed out.

But the things that interested her most were the half-dozen or so photographs of smiling young people, both male and female, in Army uniforms, and others obviously working the land. She picked up one of the latter, showing a well-built boy with dark curly hair, lifting a bundle of hay with a pitchfork, who looked vaguely familiar.

"That's me," he said, anticipating her question.

"Really? Did you grow up on a farm?"

"In a kibbutz," he said. "The first kibbutzim were organized by idealistic young Zionists, who came to Palestine at the beginning of the 20th century and dreamed of getting back to the land. There're all kinds of kibbutzim today, where they do everything, but the one I grew up in was a collective farm, very rural. We worked from morning to night, planting, sowing, harvesting the crops, milking the darn cows—the work never ended. Some kids loved it; they thrived on all that open air and sunshine, but I hated it, to be honest. So I studied hard to get into university, and I thought I had it made. But then I was drafted, just in time for the Six Day War."

"The Six Day War?" she said, slipping from his encircling arm. "What was that?"

"It was a war fought between Israel and Egypt, Jordan, and Syria, then known as the Arab Republic. The Arabs wanted to wipe Israel off the face of the map, to push the Jews into the sea. And the whole world was writing Israel's obituary.

"But President Nasser of Egypt and his cohorts were in for quite a surprise, as their Armies were unable to defend themselves against the much smaller Israel Defense Force. They went down to an ignoble defeat, and it was a turning point in Israel's history." A fleeting look of triumph lit his features for a moment, then the smile broke out again, that charming, expressive smile that went so well with his deeply tanned face and dark,

lithe grace. And he said, "On the verge
of annihilation Israel emerged, not only
victorious, but had regained Judaism's holiest
site, the Western Wall, and also occupied the
Gaza strip and more land than it had had
before."

"Did you fight in that war?" Meggie asked.

"You guessed it," he said. "That's how I
got this." His fingers traced the jagged scar
that divided his face. "I served in a tank
brigade and was hit by some shrapnel, when
I foolishly stood up in the turret to see what

was going on. Nothing very heroic on my part. But when I teach a class at Hebrew University in Jerusalem, where I'm employed as a professor of Middle Eastern affairs, the students are always fascinated by the Six Day War."

"I can see why,"Meggie said. "It sounds like a perfect example of Jack the Giant Killer— or maybe David and Goliath."

"Well, whatever." He shrugged. "It was a miraculous victory for Israel, that's for sure. But many Palestinians are still in shock at the Arabs' defeat and their own occupation, the loss of their homes. And, believe it or not, I sympathize with them a lot of the time."

"I'm sure you do. You strike me as being very fair and open-minded. I bet you're a wonderful teacher."

"Oh, I don't know about that. I just live day by day and do the best I can."

And his best was very good, Meggie was sure of that. He helped her copy down paragraphs he'd marked in the various books that he thought were pertinent, and explained the significance of some of the artifacts. She thought her mother would be thrilled at what she'd done for her. But that was hardly the case.

When she took the material over to her mother's house the next day, far from being thrilled, Mom looked bewildered and a little put out. "Why in the world would I want to write something for the newspaper?" she said. "Of course I'm interested in the Arab-Israeli conflict, especially since we've discussed it so much in the book club after reading, *The*

Lemon Tree, but people much smarter than I have written about it endlessly. Besides I'm not a writer. You're the writer in the family, honey. So why don't you dash off something for the newspaper if Marti thinks it's such a good idea?"

'Oh, Mom," Meggie sighed, "that's not the point. Professor Mandow just thought it would be interesting to have the viewpoint of an ordinary housewife in print, that's all. It's no big deal."

"Well, you're an ordinary housewife, in addition to being a very fine writer. So, I repeat, why don't *you* whip up something for Marti?"

"Oh, Mom," Meggie said again. And she was most apologetic when she met the professor that evening to return his material. "I know how much work you went to, getting all these things together, and I appreciate it, even if Mom won't co-operate. I don't know why she's acting this way really."

"Well, it's understandable. A lot of very bright people are afraid to see their words in print."

"I suppose so. She kept insisting she wasn't a professional writer and said I should write the piece, if I'm so gung-ho on the idea."

He chuckled. "Well, that's not a bad idea. How do you feel about it?"

"Oh, I don't know. I don't know anything about the situation."

"No, but I bet you're a very fast learner, and I'd be more than happy to help you."

And so it began. They met in little out-of-the-way restaurants Mouse had discovered for him, where they weren't likely to run into anyone they knew, or she went to his motel when he had a free evening. She read the books he suggested and wrote down any questions she might have, and together they explored the possibilities. Although she thought of it as something of a lark in the beginning, the more she got into the project the more it held her interest.

Marti, as he insisted she call him, just as he'd done with her mother, was an excellent teacher. He was kind and patient, and lots of fun too, and because she wanted to be available when he had some free time, she put her little girl, Robin, in day care, not without a twinge of guilt. She told Ben that she was helping her mother by researching a paper that she was writing for her book club, and being Ben he didn't question her. She continued to fulfill her job as his wife and Robin's mother, just as she'd always done, but during this strange interlude in her life she secretly lived for the stolen moments in Marti's company.

She couldn't get him out of her mind. And when the day came, a few weeks later, that she messed up on an important date in the conflict she was writing about and was close to tears, he took her in his arms to console her and kissed her. Somehow it seemed inevitable, and although she was surprised she didn't protest as his mouth moved over hers possessively, taking her to places she hadn't been in a long time.

When he finally broke the kiss, he framed her face with his hands and said, "Forgive me. I didn't mean to do that. But you're so dear, so desirable, I couldn't help myself."

"Thank you. It's all right," she said. "I have to admit, I enjoyed it too."

"Did you, my dear? That makes me very, very happy!" His teeth flashed white in that smile again, his eyes crinkled up at the corners, and he looked overjoyed and confident. "So shall we take the next step?" he said, and without waiting for an answer he took her hand and led her over to the bed. And almost before she knew it, they were undressed and making love. He was a superb lover, which didn't surprise her, and he introduced her to things she'd never even dreamed of, and she was thrilled and excited and didn't question the hours she spent in his company.

She never got around to finishing the paper they'd both been so enthusiastic about in the beginning, but it didn't matter. It seemed far more important to learn about each other. He said he wanted to know everything about her, and he listened with flattering interest to what she had to say. She told him all about her disastrous love affair with Josh and how crushed and helpless she'd felt when he left her to become a priest.

"If it had been another woman he'd fallen in love with, perhaps I could have put up some defense," she said sadly. "But I didn't have a chance against God."

No," Marti agreed. "The Almighty is all-powerful for those who believe. Of course, there's always the possibility that the young man might change his mind someday and come back, with his tail between his legs. But chances are he'd be such a different person then you might not even want him."

Not want Josh? She couldn't imagine such a possibility, no matter how long he was gone. But she felt in her bones that would never happen, and she said as much to Marti, although he insisted, "Well, you never know.

As I told you in the beginning you're the kind of woman who gets in a man's blood and makes it impossible for him to forget her. I know I'll never forget our time together. These last few glorious weeks have etched a permanent mark on my heart."

"Oh Marti," she said, touched. "Its meant a lot to me too, our time together." And she confessed how much she'd miss him when his stint as a visiting professor at Inter-Faith Theological was over.

He smiled and said he'd miss her too. "And unfortunately I have only a few more weeks," he added, his fingers touching his scar reflectively, "before I have to leave your charming city. They'll probably invite me back next year, but in the meantime, perhaps you could make a trip to Jerusalem. There're a lot of things there I could show you that you might be interested in."

"I don't doubt that for a moment."

"Good. Then let's work on it," he said. And putting out his arms he drew her close and they came together and it was just as fine as always.

They took a nap afterwards, and sometime later Meggie went in the bathroom to comb her hair before she went home. And that's when she saw it, a blue plastic shower cap lying on the floor near the sink. A bit puzzled she picked it up and went back in the bedroom. "Now, Marti, don't tell me you use this to cover your curly locks when you take a shower," she said jokingly.

He glanced at the shower cap and said, "Oh, that's not mine. It belongs to Mouse. She must have forgotten to put it away, after she took her shower this morning."

"Mouse showers here—in *your* bathroom?"

"Of course. She lives here."

"Why?"

"Why what? She's my wife."

"Your wife?" She felt exactly as if someone had kicked her hard in the stomach. "I don't understand," she said, her mind reeling with bewilderment. "I thought she was just your assistant."

"Well, she's all that—but much more besides."

"Like your pimp?"

He made a face. "I don't like that word. I think it's rather nasty."

"But it fits, doesn't it? If you see a girl you like you just have to tell Mouse, and she makes all the arrangements; right? Pretty nifty, I'd say. But tell me something, Marti, and be honest—in spite of all the sweet talk, was I just another roll in the hay to you?"

"Oh, come on," he said, putting out his hands in a pleading gesture. "I admire you tremendously, Meggie, dear. And admit it, we've had a pretty good time together, haven't we?"

"The best," she said, heading for the door.

"Where are you going?" He looked startled.

"Home. Which I should never have left. Good-bye, Marti, and thanks for everything. Its been a real eye-opening experience," she said. And she walked out, with tears streaming down her face.

CHAPTER SEVEN

The shame and humiliation she felt for her
behavior was almost more than she could
bear, and, to make matters worse, she knew
she had no one to blame for this sorry state of
affairs but herself. She had listened to Marti
Mandow's sweet nothings and followed him

blindly—mainly because she was bored. She knew that was no excuse, and just thinking of the things she'd done with him so willingly made her stomach turn, and her mind burned with the memory.

She was so filled with guilt it threatened to consume her, and trying to make amends she was nicer to Ben and spent nearly all her time with her precious Robin. She had immediately taken the little girl out of day care, telling the head teacher, whom she liked and trusted, that she'd finished the project she'd been working on and could once more devote all her time to her daughter.

"I'm glad to hear that," the teacher said, "since I've been a little worried about Robin. I'm sure it's nothing serious, but she seems more tired than usual. Have you noticed?"

"No, I really haven't," Meggie said. But she couldn't help wondering, as her conscience pricked her, if her involvement with Marti Mandow had made her somewhat oblivious to the needs of her family. She told the teacher she'd watch Robin more closely, and watch her she did, and soon came to the conclusion that the teacher was right. Her once lively little girl, who never seemed to sit still, was now perfectly content to loll on the floor and watch TV, when she wasn't falling asleep at the dinner table.

"Robin seems so pooped all the time," she told Ben. "It's as if she's run out of steam lately—I wonder why."

"Oh, I don't think it's anything to be concerned about," Ben said. "Maybe she's just settling down a bit as she gets a little older."

"I suppose," Meggie said, as she tried to convince herself it was nothing to worry about. But then Robin came down with a low-grade fever, and she decided, just to be on the safe side, to take her to Dr. Wysocki, her pediatrician, for a check-up. This was the same Timmy Wysocki, the timid little boy Meggie had known since childhood, who had been with her the first day she had stumbled, quite by accident, on the amazing crimson Stick. She had seen the Stick work its magic as it helped her to face down the schoolyard bully, the much feared Cy Barnes, who was making Timmy's life so unpleasant at times. And now this same Timmy had grown up to be a competent, successful physician, who was nice looking in a casual, easy-going way. He was also a good friend to both Meggie and Ben, and was adored by his little patients, as confirmed by Robin's big smile when she saw him.

"Ooh, hh, Dr. 'socki, Dr. 'socki," she cooed, holding out her little arms, until he picked her up and gave her a hug.

"Hello, Princess," he said. "How's my best girl today?" And Robin giggled and didn't protest when he put her on the table and started examining her a little later.

Meggie told him of her concerns, and he said he didn't think she had much to worry about, but just to be on the safe side, he added, he'd like to do some tests. And when the tests came back, instead of giving her the results over the phone, he asked her to come to his office again—and to bring Ben with her this time. She thought that rather unusual, that he wanted to see Ben in the middle of a work day, knowing how busy

Ben was. But she didn't really think too much about it until they got to his office, and she noticed that his usual cheerful, upbeat countenance looked a bit grim. He wasted no time getting to it.

"It breaks my heart to tell you this," he said, "but Robin is suffering from acute lymphoblastic leukemia."

"Good heavens!" Meggie exclaimed, instinctively reaching for Ben's hand. "That sounds pretty serious."

"It is serious," Dr. Tim said. "About as serious as you can get, I'm afraid."

"But is it treatable, curable?" Ben asked, giving Meggie's hand a reassuring squeeze.

"Sometimes. I don't know—"

"So what can we do?" Meggie asked, and suddenly a cold sweat broke out all over her body and she shivered from head to toe. It was so unexpected, so jolting, she was in a state of shock.

"Well, this is just a suggestion," Tim said. "But if Robin were my child I'd take her to Dana-Farber and Boston Children's. They're two of the best research and teaching institutions in the country that provide care for pediatric cancer patients, and they're both affiliated with Harvard Medical School. They'll take good care of our Robin, tell you what you can expect."

"But how could this have happened?" Meggie asked, struggling to regain her composure. "Robin's always been so healthy. You know that, Tim."

"I do indeed," he said. "There's no easy answer as to why things like this occur. But I know you'll face it, Meggie; you're so brave."

"Me? Brave? You must be kidding."

"Not at all. I've never forgotten how you stared down my old nemesis, Cy Barnes, when we were kids. I've often wondered where I'd be today if it hadn't been for you, Meggie."

But that wasn't me. It was the crimson Stick that saved you, she thought. But she couldn't explain that to Tim, since even though the

Stick had often intervened on her behalf, it was a secret she'd never shared with anyone. So she sat there, struggling with her emotions and squeezing her eyes tightly shut, as she pushed back the tears that threatened to spill over. *I won't cry, I have to be strong for all our sakes,* she told herself. And she wasted no time questioning Tim's suggestion.

She and Ben went home and collected Robin from the baby sitter's, packed their things, and the very next day they left for Boston. Meggie took a motel room near the hospital and enrolled Robin for treatment at the Dana-Farber/Boston Children's Center. Ben came up every Friday and stayed through the week-end.

The Center immediately started Robin on a wide variety of treatments, chemotherapy and radiation therapy being the most prevalent. Meggie knew that the hematologists and oncologists treating her daughter were among the world leaders in their specialties, and she took comfort from that. She also knew, from the gravity with which they spoke, that they considered Robin to be a very challenging case, but she had complete faith in them. All the doctors and nurses treating Robin were wonderfully kind and considerate, and Robin liked them too. Robin wasn't quite three years old yet, but she had a real personality and was adorable and so funny.

"You know what my head looks like, Mommy?" she told Meggie, when she lost all her hair. "An egg, that's what. I'm a real egg-head now. But Dr. Carter said egg-heads are okay. They're smarter than most people, and he said I'm still kind of pretty."

"You're beautiful, darling," Meggie told her. And when she ran into Dr. Carter in the hall a short time later, as she was on her way to the cafeteria to get a cup of coffee, she thanked him for being so nice to her daughter.

"It's easy being nice to that little girl. Your Robin is such a delight," the good doctor said. But for the first time Meggie noticed a kind of wariness in his eyes.

She did her best to ignore it, however, and continued to believe that Robin would soon be better. "After all, these doctors are the best," she told Ben when he came up the next week-end. "They'll fix Robin if anyone can." And she kept right on believing in miracles. Until the day Dr. Carter and his team asked her and Ben to come to his office, and told them, as gently as possible, that the time had come to take Robin home.

"But why?" Meggie asked alarmed, and she got a sudden dry taste in her mouth and a funny, quivering feeling in the pit of her stomach. "Why are you trying to get rid of her?"

"We're not," Dr. Carter said. "We've all fallen in love with Robin, she's uniquely precious—but unfortunately we can't do anymore for her."

Meggie looked at his face, sharp-boned and drawn, but still wonderfully kind and sensitive. "What are you saying?" she asked imploringly. "That Robin's case is hopeless? She'll never get better?"

"Yes." He nodded. "I'm terribly sorry, Mrs. Brown, but your little girl isn't going to make it."

This isn't happening, it's impossible! Meggie thought. Her throat was so tight that what came out didn't sound like her voice at all. But she said it. "How much longer do we have?"

The doctor sighed. "Two or three months. Six at the most, I'd say."

"My God!" Meggie whispered brokenly. She was conscious of a strange roaring in her ears, and she bit her lip to keep from screaming. She didn't remember telling Dr. Carter and his team good-bye—or packing up Robin—or what she and Ben talked about on the drive home.

It was too dreadful to think about, yet somehow she found the strength to get through those last awful days. And it wasn't all doom and gloom. For Robin's sake both she and Ben were determined to be upbeat and cheerful. They took Robin to the carousel in Elizabeth Park and smiled as she rode round and round, and held her as they went down the waterslide at Quassy Amusement Park, which she loved. They let her eat tacos and corn dogs and anything else that she wanted, and they played endless games with her and read to her by the hour.

They shared lots of happy moments, and Robin, as if sensing she had to be brave for her parents, never stopped smiling. "I'm so lucky," she said one night, as Meggie got her ready for bed. "I think it was really nice of God to give me to you."

"Oh, darling," Meggie said, hugging her, as the tears almost choked her. "Your daddy and

I are the lucky ones. We couldn't have asked for a more wonderful little girl."

"Honest?" Robin said. "Well, I'm awfully glad I please you, Mommy. I try."

"I know you do, sweetheart. And you *more* than please us," Meggie assured her. "Your daddy and I think you're pretty darn perfect." And she kissed her little daughter good-night and laid her head on the pillow, and watched as she closed her eyes and fell asleep. Then she went downstairs and told Ben what a sweet, remarkable child they had, and he agreed. But Robin never woke up.

#   #   #

Somehow Meggie got through the calling hours and the church service, and the reception afterwards that her mother insisted on having at her house. But she went through it all in a kind of daze, all the while struggling with an inner fear that if she weren't careful she'd shatter into a million jagged pieces. It was a dreary day. The morning sun had long since disappeared, leaving a sky that was a faded pale blue, almost without color. The smell of autumn was in the air. A scent of dampness and rotting leaves assailed them as they left the reception for home, the weather a fitting compliment for Meggie's mood.

"If one more person tells me that Robin is in a better place now, I think I'll bash them over the head," she told Ben.

"They're just trying to be kind," Ben said mildly. "And some folks really believe it."

"Yeah—but what do they know? Listen, Ben," hugging her arms she said stoically, "you want to know why God, or the Universe, or whatever you believe is in charge up there, decided to take Robin from us? It was to punish me, pure and simple. That's really why she died—because I sinned!"

"Oh, honey, stop torturing yourself."

"But it's true!" she insisted. "I did this really bad thing. I cheated on you, Ben. For no reason."

"I know—with that Mandow guy."

"You know about Marti?" She was so surprised she could do nothing but stare at him in stunned silence for a moment. Then she said, the words sounding as if they'd originated in some foreign language, "How *could* you know? I was so careful."

"Not very." Ben smiled wryly. "The truth is you're a pretty lousy liar, darling. All that malarkey you told me about putting Robin in day care so you'd have time to help your mother write a paper on Israeli-Palestinian relations for her book club—well, it just didn't add up. One day I asked your mom how she was coming with the research for her paper, and she didn't know what I was talking about. But in the course of the conversation she told me how impressed you were with this Professor Mandow at Inter-Faith Theological. And since I know someone who works there I did a little checking on my own, and I discovered said professor is something of a randy-dandy. Seems he has quite a reputation, as far as bowling over the ladies goes. So perhaps you couldn't resist his charms, couldn't help falling for him."

"And you don't care?"

"Ah, sweetheart—of course I care! I care terribly because I love you, more than life itself. It tore me apart to think of you in another man's arms. But I couldn't blame you because I knew in my heart that I was largely responsible.

"You weren't ready for marriage. You were still grieving over the loss of Josh, and I knew that perfectly well. And I should have waited. But I wanted you too much. So I took advantage of you in a weak moment and coerced you into marrying me. So I can't really blame you for what happened."

"Then you forgive me?"

"Lets just say we forgive each other," he smiled. Then he put his arms around her and hugged her. And he said there would never be another Robin, but they'd have more children.

How could you help loving a man like that? Meggie thought humbly. His compassion and understanding touched a core deep inside her. But she didn't believe him when he said they'd have more children. "Remember what the doctors told us when Robin was born," she reminded him. "They said it was highly unlikely I could ever get pregnant again."

He shrugged it off. "Doctors aren't infallible. They make mistakes, like other people."

And he was right. Less than a year later she gave birth to the twins, Clive and Sally, named after their grandparents. And, as if

to make up for the loss of Robin, the good

fairy, or whoever was in charge of such things,

bestowed extra blessings on the twins. They

were nice looking and even tempered, did

well in school, had loads of friends, and never

caused their parents a moment's worry. Clive

was now in his second year of law school, and

Sally was happily married with an eighteen-

month old, and was expecting another baby.

And Meggie and Ben? They had overcome

all their earlier difficulties and had enjoyed a

happy, solid marriage for the past twenty-five years. Meggie knew she couldn't have asked for a better husband and she was grateful and content, and didn't ask for anything more.

CHAPTER EIGHT

So why was her heart thumping so loudly at the thought of seeing Josh again, after all this time, that she feared it might pop right out of her chest? Her composure seemed to have completely deserted her as she changed her clothes three times, putting on three entirely different outfits, shoes included. Then, disgusted with herself, she went back to her jeans and T-shirt and stuck her feet into her well-worn sneakers.

Turning from the closet then she wet her lips and walking over to the dresser, gazed at herself, long and hard, in the mirror. She looked all right, she decided, her hair still a warm, soft brown, shot through with golden threads, thanks to the skillful help of her hairdresser. Her gray-green eyes, her best feature, were still nice and clear, and her figure svelte, since she was careful about her diet. But what difference did it make anyway, what she looked like? She was a married woman now, she reminded herself, with two grown children, a grandmother yet. But, in spite of it, the knowledge that Josh would soon be there, she'd actually see him again in the flesh, was so intoxicating it caused all her nerves to tingle. It was silly, of course, just plain crazy, but she was so thrilled she wanted to throw her arms above her head and shout.

She could hear the kitchen clock ticking, and outside the window she could see a stretch of green grass and an apple tree just starting to bloom. The flower beds near the house were filled with the crocuses she'd planted, daffodils swayed under the trees, and hummingbirds, by the dozen, darted in and out among the flowers. Glancing in the mirror again she saw a face animated with excitement and happiness, and she brushed her hair until it formed a soft, pretty halo about her face.

So she waited, and when the bell rang she ran to the door and threw it open. And there he stood, after so many years, looking absolutely marvelous, tan and fit, the few streaks of gray at his temples only adding to his attractiveness. "Meggie, girl," he cried, and he caught her close in his arms, a feeling of great warmth exuding from him, and she smelled the faint woodsy scent of his after-shave.

"Josh! Oh, Josh!" There was a wild scrambling of her pulse, her senses, her breathing—of *everything* when she saw him, and something deep inside her brought a craving so intense she thought she might die from it. She took his hand and led him into her study because it was cozier, more relaxed than the living room. And suddenly she was so euphoric she couldn't stop smiling.

He still had the same spring to his step, the same unlined, almost youthful countenance, although, on closer inspection, she noticed there were small crinkles at the corners of his eyes, and his mouth was tighter than it had once been. It was not exactly the face that she remembered, but it was still handsome and fine with its well-chiseled features and bright, sparkling eyes. Also the grin was still there and the long, lean body with its good muscles.

Meanwhile he was studying her, too. "Say, brat, you look great," he said. "*Fantastico!* How come you haven't gotten any older?"

She laughed. "Clean living, I guess."

"Sure." He smiled, a quick, lively smile. "I almost forgot. You were always a stickler for what made you feel good."

"Was I?" she said, and for absolutely no reason she remembered how she would lay beside him, after they'd made love, and feel his hand touching her breast, sending a thrill coursing all through her. She felt a little sick thinking about it, and brought her mind back to the present with a start.

"Have a seat," she said hospitably, gesturing toward the couch. "Can I get you something to eat, or drink?"

"No, thanks." He shook his head and sat down. "I had a big breakfast and got a coffee when I stopped for gas. So tell me, how's old Ben? I hear he's Mr. Success Personified, according to Dad's letters. Is that true?"

"Yes." She nodded and sat down beside him. "Ben's done very well." Not wanting to brag she didn't mention that her husband was in line for president of his company, or that most people, in the know, already considered it a done deal. "Ben will be very happy to see you, Josh."

"And I'll be happy to see him. After all, he's one of my oldest friends. But what about you, pretty girl?" He picked up her hand, lying on the seat between them, and gave it a gentle squeeze. "I hear you're turning into a real inspiration to the juvenile set, with your *No-See-Me* stories."

She laughed again and casually released her hand. "Well, not exactly. But writing the stories keeps me busy, gives me something to do. As a matter of fact," she glanced across the room to her desk, "I was working on a story when you called. People seem to like the little things and keep asking for more; I don't

know why."

"Well, why wouldn't they like them? You

were always a very talented writer."

"Think so? I never got around to completing

that novel I was always talking about."

"What? Don't tell me you never got Princess

Tahouri and her prince, Ojeni, canoodling

into marriage. But wait a sec—" he stroked

his chin, then rested his hand on his knees;

she had always been struck by that hand, the

long, sensitive fingers that looked so capable.

"Didn't Tahouri, in later versions, turn into

a high-powered woman exec named Margo

Fontaine," he added grinning, "and let's see-

-Ojeni, now known as Randolph or Ronald,

or something equally sophisticated, adored

her, but he still wasn't ready to settle down,

the fink? Correct?"

"Yep," smiling she nodded, "you've got it.

Although I must say I'm amazed that you'd

remember that silly thing. But enough about

me; what about you?" He was in mufti, she

noticed, tan slacks and a blue sports shirt open

at the neck, which surprised her. "Where's the

Roman collar?"

He shrugged. "I don't wear it."

"Not all the time?"

"Never, not anymore."

She stared at him speechless. "What

do you mean?" she said, when her voice

came back. "Don't tell me you've left the

Church?"

"Not the Church exactly, just the priesthood. I asked Rome to release me from my vows and they did. It's called laicization."

"But I don't understand. What happened?"

"Do you really want to know?"

"Yes," she said. "Tell me."

And so he began to talk, haltingly, hesitantly at first, then in a rush of words. "I loved being a priest, a Jesuit in the beginning. The Jesuits stress finding God in all things, and I truly felt I'd found God, my purpose in life, when they sent me to Africa, to Kenya. Kenya is a beautiful country with its rainforests, its lush green mountainsides, but the teeming streets of Nairobi are a different story. I was stationed in Kibera, the largest slum in sub-Saharan Africa and I worked mostly with people suffering from AIDS."

"I've heard AIDS is a scourge in Africa."

"You've heard correctly. Millions of Africans have died of that terrible disease, and countless kids have been orphaned."

"What did you do to help?"

"What did I do?" The words seemed to hang between them in little pools of air for a moment. Then he said, "Anything, and everything under the sun. Fed the hungry, found beds for the homeless, helped secure jobs for those who could still work. But my greatest achievement was starting a school, with another Jesuit, for AIDS affected kids. In order to be admitted to the school we decided that we'd only take students who had lost one or both of their parents to HIV/AIDS, and their surviving parent had to also be afflicted with the disease."

"Was the school successful?"

He shrugged. "Yes and no. We had our share of successes, but they didn't last long. The trouble was we could only keep the kids for a certain amount of time. Then we had to return them to the world, with all its temptations."

"Still, you must have been very proud of yourself, of what you'd accomplished."

"Proud of myself? Hardly." He smiled, but she could see the tension at the corners of his eyes, the sudden tightening of his mouth. "I got pretty discouraged at times. But then I found Herman."

''Herman?"

"Herman Kimetto, a five-year-old African boy. His dad, an English teacher in a junior college there, was a great admirer of Herman Melville, the author of *Moby Dick* or *The Whale,* so he named his only child after his hero. Then he and his wife, a registered nurse, both died of AIDS, leaving little Herman in care of the state. The state put him in foster care with a couple who starved and beat him with a belt, when he wet his bed, poor little kid. So he ran away, and I found him one night on the street.

"At first I thought it was just a bundle of rags tossed in this doorway," he continued. "But then the rags made a whimpering sound, and I looked closer and saw it was a child, a little boy with enormous dark eyes. 'Hello, Buddy,' I said. 'What you doing there?' And then an extraordinary thing happened. He smiled, and I forgot everything else. For I'd never seen such a smile. It was a thing of pure joy that rippled across his mouth and lit his cheeks and sent blinking little sparks of happiness dancing from his eyes, those incredible eyes like black velvet, which were truly beautiful and only accented the pathetic scrawniness of the rest of him.

"Baba," he said, which is one of many African words for dad, and he reached up and put his skinny little arms tight around my neck. "Will you take me with you?" he begged.

"Sure thing," I said, no questions asked. "And I took him home, and he became the son I never had."

"How amazinng," Meggie said. "He sounds quite precocious."

Josh nodded. "That he was. Really phenomenal. And he wasn't just bright and hard working and grateful for anything you did for him, he was also fun to be around and had a marvelous sense of humor, even as a little boy. For instance, soon after we started living together he said one night, out of the blue, "You know, Baba, it's good those bad people dressed me in rags."

"Why so?" I asked intrigued, for I was fascinated by the scope of his mind.

"Well," he laughed, "if they'd given me proper clothes you would have thought I didn't need anything and chances are you would have passed me right by. Cause you like giving folks a hand up; right, Baba?"

"Right," I said, and I laughed, too, and gave him a hug. And on that note we started our journey together. He was the kind of student every teacher dreams of, inquisitive and eager to learn, ambitious and not afraid of hard work. It didn't matter what I threw at him he'd do his best to please me, and always asked for more. He was so smart he put me to shame more than once. I had a hard time keeping up with him to tell the truth, and I was convinced he had a bright future. I figured he was Yale or Harvard material,

Princeton maybe, and I told him he should work toward going to college in the States.

"And he said, 'Sure, Baba, whatever you think. But I don't want to leave you—ever'."

"You'll never leave me, son. Even if we're separated by miles for a while, you'll always be in my heart," I assured him—and I thought how lucky I was to have found such a kid, such a sweet, wonderful boy to raise. And he kept right on being a joy, the kind of person whose very presence lit up a room.

"By the time he was sixteen he'd filled out and grown to almost six feet tall. He was a good-looking young African with smooth, chocolate colored skin and very white teeth in that bewitching smile. And he still had those big velvety eyes that drew people like a magnet and he was thoroughly engaging in every way. He never gave me a moment's worry, and I expected great things from my Herman. I felt he might have a career in the diplomatic service, or possibly teach on the college level, but he always said he wanted to be a doctor. He wanted to help find a cure for the awful disease that had killed his parents, and it never occurred to me for a moment that he wouldn't do just that. But things don't always turn out like we might hope, unfortunately." Suddenly his voice broke, and he seemed close to tears.

Meggie was almost afraid to ask, but curiosity got the better of her, and she said, "So what happened?"

Josh shrugged, and put out his hands in a helpless gesture. "Well, he vanished, that's all. One night we were having dinner and talking about which of the Ivy League colleges he should apply to first, and the next morning I noticed his bed was empty—and he was gone!"

"Just like that?"

He nodded, and the pain in his eyes was so real that she actually felt it rising in her own throat for a moment. "I looked everywhere," he said, "questioned all his friends, notified the police—but there was no trace of him. My perfect son had simply disappeared, for no reason that I, or anyone else who knew him,

273

could think of. He had seemed completely happy and well adjusted, to all appearances, and was doing well in school."

"How sad," Meggie said. There was a lump in her throat and a sudden mist before her eyes. "Did you ever find him?"

"Yes," he said, "almost two years later. I simply bumped into him on the very mean street where I'd found him originally. But he'd changed so much I hardly recognized him at first. He'd lost so much weight he was literally skin and bones and there were strange bluish patches on his face and neck. I

didn't ask any questions, but he told me he'd

been working as a prostitute, selling himself

for money to buy drugs. And now he said he

was sick; he thought it might be AIDS. And

he was right. I knew the signs.

"I'd seen enough cases to know he was

suffering from pneumocystis pneumonia, a

parasitic infection of the lungs, and a form of

skin cancer called Kaposi's sarcoma. Both are

the direct result of AIDS, and there's no cure.

So I took him home and fed him, one spoonful

at a time. It was a struggle to get food into him, but he wanted to live. He said he'd started taking drugs on the sly with his friends in high school, more as a lark than anything else, since he was sure he could handle it. But he was careless about sharing needles, and he needed more and more of the damn stuff. Then one day he realized he was hooked and couldn't stop. He was too ashamed to tell me so he ran away, my smart, lively, beautiful little boy."

She saw the agony in his face now, sharp and keen and cutting, and instinctively reaching out touched his arm. "Oh, Josh, I'm sorry, so sorry."

"Thanks," he said, putting up a hand to wipe the tears from his cheeks. "Those last few weeks were awful. He was suffering so, poor kid. Diarrhea, night sweats, high fevers—you name it, he had them all. Every morning I'd change his sheets which were wringing wet and try not to notice the swollen lymph nodes in his neck, his armpits, his groin. They were as big as pigeon eggs and at night, as I lay in bed, I'd listen to his breathing, ever more ragged and torn; it sounded like a piston. And I knew he didn't have long to live and there was nothing I could do to help him—but being Herman he tried to help me. By then his gaunt face was flushed with fever and dark purple lesions covered his entire body, and there was a strange, lost look in his eyes. But he said he loved me and he was grateful for all I'd done for him. He said he wanted to thank me, and he apologized for letting me down.

"Ah, son," I said, and all I could do was hold him tight in my arms. I could hear his breath rattling in his chest, and outside it began to rain, I remember, a cold, stinging rain that shook the windows. But as I held him, and kissed him, and told him how happy he'd made me all those years, the fear left his eyes and suddenly there was a look of calm, serene joy on his face. He died that night, two weeks short of his eighteenth birthday. It was almost a relief to let him go, he'd suffered so. But during those last sad weeks as I'd nursed him, something inside me died too. I felt a crushing sense of loneliness. What was the point of it all?"

"Oh, Josh," Meggie said again, and she could feel her ribs pushing up against her throat, making it hard to breathe. "That's the saddest story I've ever heard. But you mustn't blame yourself for Herman, and the others. You did all you possibly could."

"Maybe. But all my efforts were just a drop in the bucket, don't you see? as far as bringing about any real change. I was a failure as a Jesuit, a priest."

"Don't say that. You did your best."

"But it wasn't enough. I prayed and prayed, but prayers didn't help. I felt totally empty inside. So I left." His brows drew together in an agonized expression for a moment, and his face was a picture of such wretchedness it tore at her heart.

"You poor guy," she said, wishing there was some way to console him. "That must have been really rough for you, when you'd sacrificed so much."

"Well, it wasn't fun city, that's for sure," he admitted. "But it's okay now. I'll survive." Grinning wryly, he ran a hand over his face.

"What are you doing now?"

"I'm teaching at a prep school in New York. It's a pretty ritzy place. The kids all come from wealthy families."

"That must be quite a change from Africa."

"As different as night and day. But these kids have their share of problems. A lot of them have had to put up with their parents' messy divorces, alcoholism, drug abuse— you name it. I'm beginning to think no one escapes. But I don't get involved. I teach them as best I can, help with their studies, advise them about colleges, things like that. But when five o'clock comes I shut my desk and go home. For dinner alone, a book, or a little television maybe, then bed."

Meggie smiled. "That doesn't sound like much fun. Don't you have any social life?"

"Nope. None to speak of. It's funny, I keep remembering that summer you had the cottage at the beach. And the night I told you I was leaving. I've always felt guilty about that night, you were so hurt, so upset."

I almost died! As long as she lived she would never forget the pain of that moment when he said he was leaving. "But you said you had this calling," she reminded him. "And I was no competition against God."

"No, so I gave you up, and all you'd meant to me—the fun, the laughter, the love we shared. The very real love for this impossible dream that I could make the world a better place. But I never forgot you, Meggie, darling. You were always there in the secret places of my heart. And you're still there!"

"Oh, Josh." She was suddenly perplexed, almost frightened. "What are you saying? We can't relive the past."

"Can't we? I don't know." He turned and bending closer took her face in his hands. "Let me look at you. You're so pretty, honey, my pretty, pretty girl. I love your hair," he sighed, burying his face in it. "I always remember how it smelled so good." As he talked, mesmerizing her with his words, his fingers were sketching a line from her ear, down her throat to her breast. Then suddenly he was kissing her, and she was kissing him back. She knew it was wrong, totally inappropriate, and yet she felt a strange throbbing inside her, and a feeling of warmth, of helplessness began to take over her body. And she liked it so much she couldn't stop, nor did she want him to stop, as his lips and tongue claimed her mouth as his own. She felt joyful, strangely alive in a way she hadn't felt in years.

"Darling Meg," he said finally, taking his lips from hers. His voice was a little shaky, a little teary, and he seemed to be having trouble controlling his emotions. But he went on, in a most heartfelt way, "If you knew how I've longed to kiss you, make love to you again. When I think of all I gave up—love, marriage, children of my own, those wonderful times we shared, and for what? I feel I must have been out of my mind to have ever left you!"

"But you felt you had no choice; remember?" Her mind was reeling with confusion, and her throat felt so tight she could hardly talk. "Anyway it's a little late to think of that now, what might have been."

"Is it? I wonder. Remember what you said when I was leaving? You said if I ever changed my mind and wanted to come back, you'd always be here. Well, I have changed my mind and come back. I love you still, more than ever. So can I hold you to your promise?"

"Oh, Josh," she said again. And she saw his face, so radiant with love for her it brought tears to her eyes, and she remembered so well how it felt when they made love. She recalled how sometimes he would lie beside her, always with one hand moving over her body, whispering soft words into her ear, kissing her between words, between phrases, his arm around her waist, pulling her into him and him into her. And suddenly she wanted him so desperately she couldn't think straight. Was it too late for a second chance at love? *Well, why not?* she thought, breathless with desire. Her children were grown and didn't need her.

"I was wrong, so terribly wrong, to have ever left you," Josh was saying. "Do you remember the wonderful times we had together?"

"I remember, I remember everything," she whispered. And she realized then how hungry she was for him, and he for her. She felt a special kind of tingling in her loins and breasts that she'd almost forgotten, and she couldn't help feeling that this was what she'd been made for.

"I want you so much," she heard him murmur.

I want you too! she thought, and it was the strongest force she'd ever felt in her life.

His arms holding her close he began to kiss her face, small, soft kisses, all the while murmuring, "I love you, I love you," until she could stand it no more. She could feel the blood coursing through her veins, beating in her heart so loudly it exploded in a total loss of control, making her forget all her doubts, her caution. As she felt his mouth move to the side of her throat she groaned and wanted it all. Gently he pushed her back against the cushions and she knew he was going to make love to her, right then and there. And she wanted that, she wanted it more than she'd ever wanted anything in her life before, wanted it so much she could taste it.

'So what about it, sweetheart?" she heard him say, and he put his cheek against hers, and asked her again, "Can I hold you to your promise?"

Yes! Yes, yes, yes! her heart sang, as she snuggled against him. And suddenly the phone rang!

"Don't answer it," he said.

"Oh, it's probably just my editor, but it won't take a minute." Reluctantly she wiggled out of his arms and stood up. But her knees felt so weak she had trouble walking as she crossed the floor to her desk and picked up the phone. "Hello," she said. But it wasn't her editor, just some organization asking her to buy tickets to a concert she wasn't interested in. "No thanks," she told them. She put down the phone, and as she did so her hand touched the crimson Stick that was lying on her desk. And immediately she felt the vibrations going through her, coursing up her arms and legs at such a terrific speed she had to grab hold of the desk to keep from falling.

And suddenly she heard herself saying in this calm, clear voice, that didn't sound like her voice at all, "I'm sorry, Josh, but this isn't possible."

"What isn't possible?" he demanded, and jumping up from the couch, as if propelled by an explosive force, he started toward her, his face a picture in dismay. "You *know* you promised, Meg."

"I know, and, as I said, I'm sorry. But I'm not the same twenty-year old girl who made that promise. And you're not the same idealistic young man who set out to save the world. We're entirely different people, with totally different life experiences. You say you love me still and a part of me loves you, too, will always love you. But I'm a married woman with two grown children, a grandmother yet."

"But are you happy?" he asked, and she saw the naked longing in his eyes. And she was sad that she couldn't help him, couldn't assuage that longing. She feared that in her excitement at seeing him again she had given him the wrong impression, which filled her with guilt. But there was nothing she could do about that now.

So she said, "Yes, I'm happy," and she knew she was speaking the truth, as it came to her that she had all she needed. She was cared for, she was loved—what more could anyone ask for? She had a good marriage, a wonderful husband in Ben, dearest Ben. She remembered how he'd consoled her when

Josh left her to become a priest and she'd
wanted to die. She recalled how he'd held her
in his arms when they lost Robin and helped
her to accept their loss. And could she ever
forget how he forgave her when she betrayed
him with Marti Mandow and never held it
against her?

There was no question Ben was one-in-a-
million, and she knew she couldn't betray
him again in a futile effort to recapture all
the joys of those past, long-ago years with
Josh. What Josh was asking was just too

much and for all its lovely promises she knew doing what he yearned for would take a piece of her soul. And what had brought about this remarkable revelation, this sudden insight of truth? She felt in her heart she owed it all to *No-See-Me* and the crimson Stick, which had intervened on her behalf so many times and pointed her in the right direction. She knew such a thing didn't measure up in a rational sense, but so what? She had always believed in fairy tales, and the Stick was still vibrating frantically in her hands.

So she told Josh again that she was sorry, but it was just too late for them. "Please don't hate me."

"Ah, Meg, I could never hate you." His face was bleak with sorrow and a grimace twisted the corners of his mouth. But suddenly he smiled and reaching out caught both her wrists. "You were the best thing that ever happened to me," he said. Then letting go of her wrists he took her face in his hands. "I'll never forget you—the happiness you brought me, all the fun we shared will remain in my heart forever. And I'll love you til my dying day, but I know it's too late for me now. As you said, we can't relive the past."

"Ah, Josh, thank you for understanding."

Her eyes were bright with tears as he took his hands from her face and put his arms around her. He held her close against him for a moment, then he smiled again and gently ruffled her hair. "I knew getting you back was too good to be true. But I had to try. Give Ben my best. He's a lucky, lucky guy." Leaning down he planted a kiss on her forehead.

So under the circumstances she didn't ask him to stay for dinner, and he left soon after that. Just as he was driving off her daughter, Sally, arrived. Sally was carrying eighteen-month old Benjy on her hip and had asked her mother to watch him for her while she went to the obstetrician. Meggie shuddered to think what would have happened if Sally had arrived a little earlier and found her mother in the arms of a man not Sally's father. She thanked God she'd been spared that disaster!

"Hey, Mom, who was that attractive guy I saw just now pulling out of the driveway as I was coming in?" Sally asked.

Meggie shrugged. "Oh, just someone your father and I knew a long time ago. He was in town on business so he just dropped by to say hello."

"Oh? Well, he looked very nice."

"He is nice."

"But not as nice as Daddy?"

"No," Meggie said, and reaching out for Benjy she buried her face in his neck, in the sweet-smelling warmth of him, and buzzed him, which made him giggle. "Not as nice as Daddy."

THE END